To Ta Dark Duke

THE FALLEN DUKES

BOOK 2

A Steamy Regency Romance Novel

by

Valentina Lovelace

RUBEDIA
PUBLISHING

Disclaimer & Copyright

Table of Contents

To Tame the Dark Duke 1

    Disclaimer & Copyright 2

    Table of Contents 3

    Letter from Valentina Lovelace 5

Chapter One 6

Chapter Two 14

Chapter Three 22

Chapter Four 30

Chapter Five 38

Chapter Six 46

Chapter Seven 54

Chapter Eight 60

Chapter Nine 66

Chapter Ten 74

Chapter Eleven 83

Chapter Twelve 92

Chapter Thirteen 103

Chapter Fourteen 112

Chapter Fifteen 122

Chapter Sixteen 132

Chapter Seventeen 141

Chapter Eighteen 150

Chapter Nineteen 158

Chapter Twenty 168

Chapter Twenty-One 179

Chapter Twenty-Two 187

Chapter Twenty-Three 198

Chapter Twenty-Four 206

Chapter Twenty-Five 217

Chapter Twenty-Six 226

Chapter Twenty-Seven 233

Chapter Twenty-Eight 244

Epilogue 250

Also by Valentina Lovelace 258

Letter from Valentina Lovelace

Hello, darling!

I'm Valentina Lovelace, a hopeless romantic with a wicked imagination and a love for all things Regency. If there's a secret rendezvous, a scandal brewing, or a duke about to be undone, I'm there, probably taking notes.

I write steamy love stories where danger lurks behind every fan flutter and heroines never wait politely for permission. My stories are for readers who like their romance with sharp tongues, slow teases, and absolutely no chill.

Off the page, I'm raising two tiny, adorable, future scandal-makers, believing I'm in control of the household (I'm not), pretending tea is a personality trait, and occasionally convincing my husband to "act out" plot research.

If you're into bold women, bad decisions, and ballroom gossip turned foreplay — welcome. I've been expecting you!

Till our next whispered word,

Chapter One

Lady Charlotte Montclair set down her quill and regarded the ink-splattered page with a wistful smile.

How many letters were there now? Twenty? Thirty?

Enough that her desk drawer had become a trove of secrets bound in wax and ribbon, for they were all confessions she dared not speak aloud, sentiments she could only entrust to Edmund Larke's elegant hand.

What foolish happiness his words brought her. Lines of poetry so tender, so understanding, they seemed to draw the very marrow of her soul onto the page. At last, someone had seen *her*, not Lady Charlotte the dutiful sister, nor the pious spinster hiding behind charitable causes, but Charlotte herself, with her secret longings and unspoken dreams.

One day soon, she told herself, she would no longer have to hide. Edmund would come. He would walk through the great doors of Hawthorne House, bow to her brother, and with the gravity of a gentleman declare his honourable intentions. And then... then she might live as other women did with a husband who cherished her, a household of her own, a life no longer bound to waiting.

The thought swelled in her chest until she could scarcely contain it. Folding the sheet with careful precision, Charlotte pressed her seal into the warm wax and held it a moment longer than necessary, as though to capture the promise within.

"Safe with you," she whispered, as if Edmund himself could hear her.

She slipped the letter into her reticule, tucked beside her prayer book and a sprig of lavender. To the world, it would seem only another simple note sent on behalf of her charities. No one, not even Nicholas, who fancied himself so perceptive, would guess how fiercely her heart beat within those modest folds of paper.

Charlotte tied the ribbons of her bonnet beneath her chin with fingers steadier than her heart. She smoothed the folds of her pelisse, which was pale blue trimmed in ivory, and regarded her reflection in the looking glass. Composed and serene, she was the very picture of dutiful propriety. No one would suspect she carried a secret so precious, it felt at times like a flame hidden beneath her ribs.

Then, a brisk rap upon the door startled her from her thoughts.

"Come in," Charlotte called, gathering her gloves from the writing table.

The door swung open to reveal Aunt Beatrice, upright and formidable as ever. Her silver-streaked hair was arranged in a tidy coiffure that seemed impervious to weather or time. Her sharp and assessing eyes swept Charlotte from bonnet to hem.

"And where, my dear, are you bound so early in the day?" Aunt Beatrice asked with curiosity.

Charlotte hesitated only a breath before replying, "To the village. I have a letter to send." However, she could not stop the blush that crept up her neck.

"Ah." A knowing gleam lit her aunt's eyes. She crossed the chamber with a rustle of skirts and perched herself on the edge of the bed, clearly in no hurry to depart. "Our family does seem unusually fond of correspondence these days. First Nicholas and now you. I begin to wonder whether you are writing a love letter."

Charlotte blinked, torn between laughter and indignation. "Aunt!"

"Oh, do not bristle so," Aunt Beatrice said, patting her hand. "I merely tease. Lydia is as dear to me now as though she were my own daughter. Indeed, I cannot imagine Hawthorne House without her." Her smile softened as the sharpness in her tone dissolved into genuine fondness. "But you must admit that your brother's choice took us all by surprise. Society will never cease to chatter about it."

Charlotte's lips curved despite herself. "And yet, I daresay, Nicholas is far happier for it."

"Quite so," Aunt Beatrice conceded. "Which is why I shall not protest should you decide to follow in his footsteps. Though…" Her brows lifted archly upon those words. "If you intend to shock us, do at least have the courtesy to find a man with a tolerable fortune."

Charlotte forced a laugh, though her cheeks were still warm beneath her aunt's scrutiny. If Aunt Beatrice only knew the truth behind the folded parchment in her reticule, she would not jest so lightly.

So, she slipped on her gloves, smiling with as much composure as she could muster.

"You needn't worry yourself, Aunt," she said lightly. "My errand is a dull one. There are no scandalous secrets to be wrung from it, I assure you."

Aunt Beatrice narrowed her eyes in mock suspicion, though her lips twitched with amusement. "Mm. That is what your brother once told me when he galloped off to London on *business*. He returned with a wife. Mark me, Charlotte, I am growing quite expert at detecting mischief in Montclair blood."

"I leave the mischief to Nicholas," Charlotte replied, gathering her reticule. "Good day, Aunt."

Before her aunt could further detain her, Charlotte swept from the chamber and down the stairwell. She could feel her pulse quickening with each step. The manor's marble hall gave way to the crisp air of morning, and soon she was mounted in her carriage, with the familiar road winding toward London.

The streets on the outskirts of town lay quiet beneath a soft autumn haze. Shopkeepers arranged baskets of apples and bolts of fabric, a blacksmith's hammer rang faintly in the distance, and children darted through narrow lanes with shrill laughter. Yet few looked her way, and fewer still recognized her. Years of absence from society's whirl had rendered Lady Charlotte Montclair a ghost of sorts. Her name was remembered more readily in whispers than in greetings.

To be quite honest, it was oddly liberating. To walk unremarked upon, to vanish into the common current of village life, felt more like freedom than disgrace.

At the post office, she slid her sealed letter across the counter, her breath catching as the clerk tucked it into a waiting satchel bound for Bath. Her heart thudded with the certainty that, within days, Edmund would read her words, her hopes, her devotion. Perhaps this letter would be the one that would summon him at last.

But she did not linger. To do so would draw questions, and Charlotte had long ago perfected the art of slipping from scrutiny.

Her steps carried her on to St. Bartholomew's, the modest stone church that had become the centre of her quiet labours, outside the confines of Hawthorne. The air smelled faintly of beeswax and woodsmoke, and the echo of her footsteps accompanied her as she crossed the nave to the vestry, where a stack of parcels awaited her attention. Bolts of cloth, baskets of bread, jars of preserves, they were all the makings of relief for those whose lives knew little of comfort.

Charlotte loosened her bonnet and set to work, pinning up her sleeves with practiced efficiency. The vestry was already alive with the scent of flour and wool, the air cool despite the faint autumn sunlight streaming through the high windows.

"Careful with that, Meg," she said gently as one of the village girls struggled with a heavy basket of bread loaves. "If the crusts break, they'll grow stale before the week is out."

"Yes, my lady." Meg flushed, lowering the basket more carefully this time.

Charlotte smiled in encouragement before turning to the other girl, Anna, who was folding blankets into neat piles. "Those are for the orphanage, Anna. See that each one has a lavender sachet tucked inside. Children sleep better when comfort is close at hand."

Anna's eyes brightened. "Like the one you gave me last winter, my lady? It smelled so fine I kept it in my pocket for months."

"Just so," Charlotte replied, a quiet warmth filling her chest. "We must not think only of keeping bodies warm, but hearts as well."

She moved to the small desk tucked against the vestry wall and unfolded her list, running a finger down the carefully inked columns.

"Widow Davies is to have her pension today," she murmured, half to herself, half to the room. "And the poorhouse must have its stores of candles before the evenings grow too dark. I will not have the poor stumbling about in shadows."

Meg ventured a shy smile. "It is good of you, Lady Charlotte. Most ladies wouldn't bother themselves with such things."

Charlotte looked up from her ledger, her gaze softening. "Most ladies are occupied otherwise. But I have time, and time is a gift, Meg. One must use it wisely."

The girls nodded solemnly, and Charlotte returned to her lists, though her thoughts wandered as her pen traced names. Here, in the dust and quiet bustle, she shed the weight of her family name. No one cared that she had once been a darling of London society, nor that whispers now cast her as a pious recluse.

Needing another ledger, Charlotte slipped toward the door that led to the storeroom. There, in the back storage room, a group of townsmen were stacking firewood and shifting crates brought in by a cart. She stepped lightly, skirts brushing the floor as she reached for the door handle, then froze.

Her name drifted to her through the half-open door.

"Yes, Lady Charlotte Montclair," a man said, and the syllables stretched with amusement. "Poor, prim creature thinks herself clever, but she swallowed every word I gave her."

Charlotte's breath stilled in her throat, but she still tried to suffocate it with her hand on her lips. The voice... she *knew* it. Smooth, lilting, with that faintly theatrical cadence that had enchanted her in his letters.

It was *Edmund.*

Another man chuckled. "Is it true, then? You've been courting her?"

"Courting?" Edmund gave a sharp laugh. "Hardly. I wrote her a sonnet or two, strung some moonlit phrases together. She lapped it up, like a kitten after cream. Foolish, desperate thing, ready to fall into any man's arms, so long as he promised her devotion."

The words struck her like a blow. Charlotte pressed her back against the wall, gripping the stone as though it alone could keep her upright.

"You mean to wed her, then?" the second man pressed.

"Wed her?" Edmund scoffed while his voice was full of contempt. "I've no wish to yoke myself to a spinster nearly on the shelf. But a Montclair fortune?" His tone turned sly. "Ah, that I might have endured for a season. She's naive enough to believe a gentleman poet would risk his heart for her. Imagine, Lady Charlotte, dreaming of marrying a commoner. What a jest!"

The men laughed in a sound that was rough and merciless, echoing through the storeroom.

She staggered back from the door, her heart pounding so loudly she feared they might hear it. All the warmth of the church, the comfort of her work, seemed to drain away, leaving only a cold hollowness spreading through her chest.

She could not stay... not a moment longer.

Turning swiftly, Charlotte gathered her skirts and fled down the vestry corridor.

The girls called after her. "My lady? Are you unwell?"

But she could not answer, nor could she risk her voice betraying the anguish tearing her apart. She pushed open the church's side door, stumbling into the pale daylight.

The air struck cold against her cheeks, and only then did she realize they were wet. Tears coursed freely, blurring the familiar outlines of the village street as she hurried away. She cared nothing for who might see her, though few glanced up at all. Lady Charlotte Montclair had so long vanished from society's view that even her distress went unnoticed.

Her carriage waited where she had left it. Climbing inside, she sank into the corner. Her chest rose and fell in broken sobs, grief and humiliation warring with each shuddering breath. Edmund's cruel and mocking words rang in her ears, stripping bare every hope she had dared to nurture.

Foolish. Desperate. Naive.

The wheels jolted into motion, carrying her back toward Hawthorne House. Outside the window, the countryside blurred into a wash of autumn gold and fading green. Inside, Charlotte bowed her head into her gloved hands and let the tears fall unchecked, each one a testament to a heart betrayed.

By the time the manor gates came into view, her eyes burned and her throat ached with the force of her weeping. She knew she had to compose herself before facing Nicholas or Lydia, but in that moment, all she could feel was the hollow ache of a dream shattered, an ache so sharp it seemed it might never leave her.

Chapter Two

A month had passed since Charlotte Montclair's heart had shattered in a church vestry, and in that month, she had learned the art of silence, of stillness, of *stone*.

Once, she would have trembled with anticipation at the thought of rejoining society after so long an absence. Once, she would have whispered secret hopes into her looking glass, wondering whether love might find her. But that Charlotte was gone, buried with her foolish letters and girlish dreams.

Now she found herself sitting before her dressing table, her face reflected back at her in the tall oval glass. The maid fastened her gown with brisk efficiency. It was ivory silk with a modest train, almost severe in its elegance. Charlotte had chosen it deliberately. Not the frothy pastels of youth, nor the girlish fripperies she once adored. Ivory was austere, unyielding, unromantic.

Her hair, coiled into a smooth chignon, gleamed like spun gold beneath the comb of pearls her maid secured. No ringlets tumbled loose, no playful curls framed her face. There was nothing to soften her.

Charlotte regarded the woman in the mirror. She scarcely knew her. Her eyes, which were once bright with hope, were cool now, narrowed with determination. Her mouth, once quick to smile, pressed in a line of composure. She looked as though she had been carved, each feature honed into restraint.

"Very fine, my lady," her maid murmured as she adjusted the fall of the gown's sleeve.

Charlotte inclined her head, but her thoughts remained inward. Very fine indeed, but for what purpose? She did not seek admiration, nor affection. She sought a name, a title, a shield against the humiliation of her own gullibility. If marriage must be her lot, then let it be a union of duty. Let her stand secure as a duchess or marchioness, respected if not loved.

Never loved.

The words coiled bitterly in her chest. Love was folly. Love was weakness. Love was the hand that struck her down and left her gasping in the dust. She had believed in sonnets and promises, and for her belief she had been mocked, deceived, ruined in all but name.

Not again.

She rose from her seat, with the ivory silk whispering about her ankles like the rustle of armour. Her maid stepped back, curtsying as Charlotte drew on her gloves with steady fingers.

"I am ready," Charlotte said in a voice that was clear, composed, and utterly devoid of tremor.

Exactly an hour later, she found herself standing in Lady Evelyn Whitmore's ballroom, which glittered with the strength of a thousand watchful eyes. The hum of conversation rose and fell with the music, punctuated by the rustle of fans and the sharp titter of laughter.

It was just as Charlotte remembered... and just as dull.

She moved through the crush with her brother Nicholas at her side. Eyes turned toward her. She could feel them curious, calculating, assessing. For years, she had been absent, spoken of in whispers as a reclusive spinster or, worse, a woman fallen so far as to be of no consequence. Now she stood in their midst again, unveiled, and their stares carried the bite of judgment.

"Lady Charlotte," one of her old companions drawled as they met in passing. The woman's smile was polished, her eyes anything but. "We had begun to think you meant never to return."

Another leaned close, fan fluttering as though to mask her words. "And to return now, of all times. Why, the seasons have left you quite behind, have they not?"

Charlotte inclined her head, lips curving in a cool approximation of a smile. Their voices, once so dear to her, seemed shallow now; mere thin, brittle things that could not pierce her newly forged armour.

Let them whisper.

Let them measure her against their silken standards. She had no need of their approval.

She drifted on, her gaze seeking the familiar instead. At the far end of the room, she spied her sister-in-law, Lydia, as she conversed with Sebastian Graves and his wife, Emma. Lydia spotted her first, her smile blooming with such warmth that Charlotte's guard wavered for just a heartbeat. Lydia held out a hand as Charlotte approached.

"There you are," Lydia said. "I was beginning to despair of your finding us in this crowd of peacocks."

Sebastian chuckled. "We do rather outshine the plumage, don't we, Emma?"

"Oh, most certainly," Emma said with a grin, slipping her arm through Charlotte's. "I've missed you terribly, Charlotte. You've been too long away."

Charlotte felt the tightness in her chest ease. Here, at least, she was not measured and found wanting. Here she was not a relic or a curiosity, but a sister, a friend. She allowed herself the faintest of genuine smiles.

"It is good to be back," she said simply, though the words carried a weight none of them could know.

For while the ball unfolded around her in all its predictable patterns--the same gossip, the same music, the same hollow flirtations--Charlotte stood apart. She was no longer the girl who had once ached to belong to this glittering world. She would endure it, yes. She would even master it. But she would never again bow to it.

Charlotte was still standing with Lydia and Emma as a cluster of ladies descended, their tones syrupy with praise.

"Duchess, you must tell us, where did you have that gown made?" one asked Lydia, brushing her gloved hand across the delicate embroidery.

"And the cut of your sleeve! Simply divine," another chimed in. "It is the talk of the room."

Lydia's cheeks flushed, though her smile remained poised. "You flatter me. They are my own designs. I could not ask others to wear what I would not wear myself."

A ripple of admiration passed through the group. Charlotte felt a pang that was not envy but pride. Lydia had fought hard for her place in this world, and now it was hers by merit as much as by marriage.

As the ladies drifted away, Lady Evelyn Whitmore herself glided near. Her gown shimmered like midnight silk, and suddenly, her fan snapped open with the crispness of a blade. She leaned in conspiratorially, and Charlotte could not take her eyes off of the woman's overly rouged lips.

"My dears, you cannot have failed to notice," she whispered, her eyes darting toward the great doors. "The Duke of Duskbourne has arrived."

Charlotte's brow furrowed before she could school her expression. "The Duke?"

"Indeed," Lady Whitmore purred, clearly savouring the stir she had caused. "Lord Cassian Oberon himself, here in my ballroom. He has not set foot in such a gathering in nearly a decade. Grief, they say... poor man. Since the death of his wife, he has cloistered himself away at that great moorland fortress of his. But..." She flicked her fan open again. "He makes an exception for charity. A noble soul, though far too cold for my tastes."

Nicholas approached in time to catch the end of her remark. His tone was dry. "Coldness, Lady Whitmore, is preferable to the heat of idle gossip."

Lady Whitmore only laughed, unoffended, but Charlotte barely paid attention to them, because her eyes were focused on something else. Or rather, on *someone* else.

The crowd parted just enough to grant her a clear view: a tall man standing near the edge of the dance floor, where conversation was at its thickest. He was enduring the attentions of several gentlemen and no small number of ladies, yet his posture betrayed indifference. His expression was cut from marble—just like hers. He appeared polite, but bored, his gaze drifting as though none of what he saw held the faintest interest.

Charlotte studied him. A dark, striking figure with angular features and a gravity that seemed to bend the air around him. He did not laugh, did not smile, not even when a lady brushed closer than courtesy required. His grey and glacial eyes missed nothing, yet warmed for no one.

"Every woman here is dreaming of becoming the next Duchess of Duskbourne," Lady Whitmore remarked, fanning herself briskly at Charlotte's side. "A duke widowed these many years, with no heir. He is, of course, the perfect match." She leaned in, lowering her voice in scandalized delight. "But the trouble is, he will not look at any of them. Not truly. They say he has no heart left to give. Not since his poor Eleanor."

Nicholas gave a snort of disdain and turned away, unwilling to indulge her further, but Charlotte's eyes did not leave the Duke.

No heart. No interest. No need of love.

And suddenly, as though a veil had lifted, Charlotte saw it clearly. *He* was the solution she had been seeking all these weeks.

Cassian Oberon, Duke of Duskbourne, was precisely what she needed.

He was a man scarred by love, who would never again risk it. He was also a man above reproach in station, whose title would erase whispers of her spinsterhood. She was too old for the foppish heirs who sought pliant girls of seventeen. At six and twenty, she was steady and practical and would best suit a man who desired nothing but duty.

It was perfect: a marriage of convenience, a union of necessity. He would gain a wife who asked for nothing more than respect, and she would gain the shield of his name and the freedom to silence society's wagging tongues.

There would be no passion, no sonnets and pretty lies, and most importantly, no heartbreak.

Charlotte's lips curved with resolve. She would not wait. She would seize what security was left for her.

Charlotte scarcely heard Lydia's voice beside her, nor Emma's teasing remark about some hapless suitor attempting a bow too deep. Their laughter reached her as though muffled through water. Her gaze remained fixed on the man across the ballroom, the Duke of Duskbourne, standing solitary amidst the crowd.

Emma nudged her. "Charlotte, you've not heard a word, have you? I was saying I would sooner throw myself into the Serpentine than endure such clumsy devotion. Don't you agree?"

"Mhm," Charlotte murmured, gaze still lingering on the Duke as he shifted away from the crowd. Without ceremony, without excuse, he began to cross the ballroom toward the adjoining hall, disappearing into the corridor's shadows.

Charlotte's heart gave a sudden, decisive lurch. This was her chance.

"I must excuse myself," she said quickly, not waiting for Lydia's questioning look or Nicholas's raised brow.

She gathered her skirts and slipped into the hall as quickly as she could. The air here was cooler, the candlelight dimmer, and her pulse impossibly loud in her ears.

She saw him turn down a side passage, one that led toward the retiring rooms. His stride was unhurried and utterly unconcerned with who might follow.

Drawing a breath that scorched her lungs, Charlotte followed.

The door clicked shut behind him. She stopped in front of the door, hesitating for a single moment, then she pushed it open, stepping into a panelled chamber perfumed faintly with tobacco and brandy: the gentlemen's retiring room.

The Duke had just removed his gloves when he stilled. Slowly, he turned, his tall frame casting a long shadow. His eyes fell upon her, cold and assessing.

"You are in the wrong room, my lady," he told her, sounding both surprised and annoyed.

Charlotte lifted her chin, summoning the stone she had become. "Perhaps. But I have a proposition for you, Your Grace."

For the first time, something flickered in his gaze. It was not surprise, nor amusement, but the faintest narrowing of interest. His eyes swept over her once, almost as if in an effort to assure himself that she was a being made of flesh and blood, and not a ghost. Then, they settled back upon her face.

And the chamber seemed to hold its breath as silence stretched between them.

Chapter Three

Cassian Oberon, the Duke of Duskbourne, was able to relish his solitude for only one brief moment before the mysterious woman who had followed him into the retiring room boldly announced that she had a proposition for him.

Cassian stilled, regarding her more closely. Fire burned in her gaze, as well as an unmistakable defiance that cut through the polite blandness of every other woman he had endured tonight.

Striking, he thought. Though not in the manner of delicate beauties. There was steel in this one.

His mouth curved into the barest shadow of a smile, which was more sardonic than warm. "If anyone were to find us here alone, my lady... could you imagine what they would say? The gossip would be relentless."

Her reply felt like an earthquake. "My reputation is already tarnished, Your Grace. I have little left to lose."

Something in her tone caught him: honesty sharpened to a blade. It was not a trait easily embodied by a woman of the ton, who so often had to resort to manipulations and lies.

"Then, firstly, you could tell me the name of the woman so reckless with her reputation."

She inclined her head, composed as though she stood in a drawing room rather than a gentlemen's retreat. "Lady Charlotte Montclair."

Cassian's eyes narrowed. The name stirred a memory, which was clouded with whispers from clubs and drawing rooms years ago. A duke's sister, once seen at every season, then vanished so completely that tongues wagged with speculation.

Some said she had taken ill, others that she had turned pious and withdrawn.

Yet here she was. Not frail, not hidden away. Bold, steady, and very much alive.

For the first time in years, Cassian felt the faintest flicker of intrigue.

"I will speak plainly, Your Grace." Her voice did not falter. "I propose marriage."

He stilled, the glove in his hand now completely forgotten.

She continued, calm and unyielding, like an army general proposing the best plan of attack. "A marriage of convenience. No affection required. You would be spared the endless parade of matchmaking mothers and the expectations of romantic folly. And I would, in turn, be freed from the ignominy of spinsterhood and the shadows of my past. A union of duty, nothing more."

Her words struck with the precision of a clean blade, unembellished and utterly merciless in their clarity.

Cassian felt his brow arch, though his expression remained otherwise inscrutable. "You propose marriage," he repeated, the syllables edged with disbelief.

"Yes." She did not blink. "You are a duke who does not wish to be hounded by society's expectations. I am a lady who no longer believes in love. Between us, there would be no risk of disappointment."

Her eyes, so fiercely blue, held his without wavering. Defiance and composure twined together, and Cassian, who had spent years mastering the art of silence, found himself regarding her with a kind of dark fascination. A woman proposing to him, in such an unflinching manner, as though it were the most natural transaction in the world. He had never seen its like.

At last, Cassian allowed himself the smallest exhale of laughter, albeit cold and humourless. "You astonish me, Lady Charlotte." His gaze swept her once again. "Most women who seek a duke would at least feign a sonnet or two."

"I have no interest in sonnets," she said simply.

For a long moment, Cassian said nothing. He only studied her, this woman who had walked straight into a gentlemen's retiring room and delivered a proposal as though she were striking a bargain over land.

Before he could stop himself, he closed the space between them. The faint rustle of her skirts brushed the silence, and her breath caught, yet she did not retreat. Intrigue sharpened his curiosity, and with deliberate precision, he reached out and tilted her chin upward.

Her eyes met his, fire answering steel.

"Do you have the faintest notion," he murmured incredulously, "how absurd this is? Reckless, even. For a lady to follow a man into such a place... *alone.*" He let the word linger. "It invites ruin."

Her chin did not waver beneath his hand. "I told you, Your Grace. My reputation is already tarnished. I have little left to lose."

Something twisted in his chest at the cool certainty in her tone. It was a glaring echo of a pain he had long buried. He released her at once, as though burned.

"You should not have come here," he said, colder now, as he drew back. His eyes swept over her once more, searching for weakness and finding only iron.

Without another word, he turned, his stride measured as he pulled open the door and stepped back into the dim corridor. The ballroom's music floated faintly from beyond, but Cassian heard only the echo of her voice and the clarity of her audacity.

A proposal without affection. A marriage without risk.

It was absurd and reckless... *unthinkable.*

And yet, despite himself, he found his thoughts lingering on Lady Charlotte, on her defiance and on her daring to speak to him as no one else had in years.

By the time he reached the hall again, Cassian realized with grim irritation that Lady Charlotte Montclair had carved herself a place in his mind.

***

"You will scarcely believe what I am about to tell you," Cassian said, his tone so dry it drew Gideon's full attention at once.

Lord Gideon Harrow, who was sprawled in his chair at White's with a brandy glass dangling carelessly between his fingers, raised a brow.

"Coming from you, Oberon, I should prepare myself for a tale of crop rotations or a speech on the corn laws."

Cassian's lips pressed into a thin line. "A woman proposed to me."

The brandy nearly sloshed over Gideon's hand. He sat upright with a bark of laughter that earned a scandalized glance from a nearby earl. "A woman?"

"Yes."

"Proposed marriage?" He asked, as if anything else was far more reasonable.

"Yes."

Gideon leaned forward, grinning with unabashed delight. "The stoic and untouchable Cassian Oberon, Duke of Duskbourne, was caught unready by a lady with more nerve than sense? God help me, tell it slowly, I mean to savour every word."

Cassian's grey eyes narrowed, but against his will, he felt the words pressing forward. He recounted the entire story with grim precision: the retiring room, the sudden intrusion, the steady fire in her eyes, and her astonishing declaration. He ended with a shake of his head, as though even in retelling, he found it unbelievable.

"She asked for a marriage without affection," Cassian said at last, emphasizing the final part. "Convenience. Duty. As though such a thing could be arranged like the purchase of a horse."

For a long moment, Gideon simply stared. Then he threw back his head and laughed as only rakes did, richly and without shame. "By God, there are such women! And she sought *you* of all men? I am astounded, Oberon. Positively astounded. Most ladies I know would faint dead away before daring so much as a glance at you."

"It was reckless," Cassian said curtly. "If anyone had discovered her in that room alone with me, her reputation would have been in tatters."

"And yet she came," Gideon countered, as his eyes gleamed with mischief. "And spoke plain as day. You must admit, it takes courage. Or desperation. Perhaps both."

Cassian's jaw tightened. He had thought the same, though he refused to say it aloud. "It was absurd," he said instead. "Unthinkable."

Gideon swirled his brandy, the smile still tugging at his mouth. "Unthinkable, perhaps. But I cannot recall the last time anything unsettled you, Oberon. And now..." He leaned back, studying his friend with rakish amusement. "Now you are telling me this story at White's, which means the lady has succeeded in doing what half of London has failed to do: occupy your mind."

Cassian said nothing, but the faintest flicker crossed his eyes.

Gideon's grin widened. "Well, well... I do believe I should like to meet this Lady Charlotte Montclair."

Cassian set his glass down with a sharp click. "You do not understand. She is dangerous."

Gideon arched a brow, wholly unbothered. "Dangerous? She is not a highwayman, Oberon, merely a lady with more fortitude than most."

"Fortitude?" Cassian's voice carried an edge. "I would call it foolishness. That kind of directness... it unsettles propriety. It unsettles..." He stopped himself short.

"Unsettles *you*," Gideon supplied smoothly, and now, there was a sly grin curving his mouth. "And that, my friend, is why you call her dangerous. Admit it, she is unlike anyone you have encountered."

Cassian's jaw tightened. "Too unlike. She does not shrink. She does not flatter. She demands."

"And precisely therein lies her merit," Gideon countered, leaning forward with a gleam in his eye. "A woman who

27

demands nothing of your heart, Oberon, is the very woman you require. She is not some simpering debutante. She would not ensnare you with sonnets and sighs. A duchess who will not ask for love, now that is perfection itself."

Cassian's hand curled around his glass, though he did not drink. Gideon's words struck too close to the truth, to the quiet thought he had been fending off since last night: a union without affection, without risk. Safety draped in scandalous boldness.

"It is reckless," he repeated, though the force behind his protest was waning.

"Reckless?" Gideon smirked. "Perhaps. But is it not better than the alternative? Every ambitious mother in London thrusting her daughter beneath your nose until you are forced to marry some pliant girl who will flutter her lashes and expect your devotion?"

Cassian's lips pressed into a line. He could picture it too easily: simpering youth, false tenderness, the slow suffocation of demands he could not give.

No. He would not relive such folly.

Gideon tipped his glass toward him, speaking with utter earnestness. "Consider it, Oberon. For once, fate may have handed you precisely what you need."

Cassian looked away, staring into the amber liquid in his own untouched glass. Silence stretched, taut as wire.

At last, he exhaled slowly. "Very well. I will arrange a private meeting with her. Tomorrow."

Gideon's grin was swift and triumphant. "Excellent. I should very much like to be there when you respond to her proposal."

Cassian shot him a withering look, but Gideon only laughed.

Still, even as the din of White's swelled around him once more, Cassian could not shake the image of fire-blue eyes meeting his with fearless resolve.

Dangerous, yes. Absurd, yes.

Yet tomorrow, he would see her again.

And the thought both unsettled and intrigued him beyond bearing.

Chapter Four

Charlotte unfolded the letter for the third time that morning. Her gloved fingers were busy smoothing the parchment, though the words were already seared into her memory.

His Grace, the Duke of Duskbourne, will wait upon Lady Charlotte Montclair at Hawthorne, at noon.

She stared at the lines as if they might vanish should she blink. That he had considered her outrageous proposal at all was remarkable. That he had replied, civilly, with the cold brevity of a man confirming a business appointment, was near unthinkable.

Her heart gave a treacherous flutter. She pressed the letter closed and set it beside her teacup, forcing her face into composure just as Nicholas strode into the parlour.

"You are quiet this morning," her brother observed, pausing to pour himself a cup of tea. "And when you are quiet, Charlotte, it is either because you are plotting or because you are hiding something."

Charlotte lifted her chin, feigning indifference. "Not everything requires a plot, Nicholas. Some mornings are simply... quiet."

He lowered himself into the chair opposite hers, eyeing her with the unerring gaze that had made him formidable in both Parliament and his own household.

"Mhm. Yet you are staring at that letter as if it contains the fate of the nation."

Charlotte slid the parchment toward the edge of the table, stacking it neatly with other correspondence. "Merely a charitable inquiry."

Nicholas's brow arched. "From whom?"

She sipped her tea, refusing to answer. If she were honest, she would have confessed that Cassian Oberon's cool grey eyes had not left her mind since the night of the ball and that the memory of his gloved hand tilting her chin upward had lit some strange, unwelcome fire in her chest. She might have admitted that though his bluntness grated, though he seemed the last man in England capable of tenderness, she still could not forget the sensation of standing beneath his scrutiny.

But honesty was dangerous.

And besides, she reminded herself fiercely, he would not truly wish to marry her. He had only agreed to meet because propriety demanded a refusal be delivered in person; no more, no less.

"Charlotte," Nicholas pressed, in a tone that was softer and more fatherly. "What trouble are you walking into?"

She forced a small smile, the kind she had perfected through long practice. "Nothing that need concern you, brother."

Nicholas frowned, clearly unconvinced, but before he could press further, a knock on the parlour door interrupted them.

"Yes?" Charlotte called out impatiently, and a moment later, the door opened.

"The Duke of Duskbourne, my lady," the maid announced, her eyes flicking curiously between Charlotte and Nicholas before retreating with a curtsy.

Nicholas's head snapped toward her, his dark brows lifting. "The Duke of *what?*"

Charlotte smoothed her gown, though her pulse thrummed at her throat. "Duskbourne."

He stared at her. "And you knew something of this?"

She folded her hands neatly in her lap, lifting her chin with careful composure. "You will find out everything in a moment."

"Charlotte—" His voice carried a warning, edged with disbelief.

She met his gaze steadily, though her insides quaked. "Trust me, Nicholas."

It was a plea as much as a command. Her brother's frown deepened, but he exhaled heavily and leaned back in his chair. Only the tension in his shoulders betrayed his unease. He obviously did not like it. In fact, she knew he *hated* not knowing, hated seeing her full of secrets, but his affection for her was stronger than his impatience.

"Very well," he said at last, though the words sounded dragged from him. "But God help this duke if he means to trifle with you."

Charlotte's lips curved faintly, though her heart felt anything but light.

If only you knew, Nicholas, it is I who means to trifle with him.

The door opened again, and there he was. Cassian Oberon entered the parlour with the silent command of a man accustomed to being obeyed. Tall, dark, and striking, his presence seemed to fill the space before he had uttered a single word. His coat was black, severe as ever, and his cravat was flawlessly knotted. Those grey eyes swept the room, missing nothing, yet also betraying nothing.

"Your Grace," Nicholas said, rising at once with the formality due to rank, though his voice carried a cautious edge.

Duskbourne inclined his head, grave and unreadable. "Hawthorne." His gaze shifted to Charlotte, lingering there with that same disconcerting weight as the night of the ball. "Lady Charlotte."

Her composure wavered under the intensity of his regard, but she forced her spine straight and her voice steady. "Your Grace. Welcome to Hawthorne House."

Duskbourne inclined his head back to Nicholas. "I thank you for receiving me, Hawthorne. I trust Hawthorne House prospers under your care."

Nicholas gave a short nod that meant nothing. "We fare well enough, Your Grace. Though I admit, I am at a loss as to what occasion could bring you here. You are not known for your visits to society or anywhere beyond your own estates."

A pause blossomed, thick with meaning.

The Duke's gaze flicked once to Charlotte, then back to her brother. "I am here to speak with Lady Charlotte."

Nicholas stiffened. "Then speak with her. Whatever you have to say, it is for my ears as well."

Charlotte's breath caught, but the Duke betrayed not the slightest hesitation. He inclined his head as if Nicholas' words were of no consequence. "Very well. Then I shall be direct." His eyes returned to Charlotte, almost unblinking. "Lady Charlotte, I propose marriage."

The silence that followed was deafening. Nicholas inhaled sharply. "You what?"

The Duke did not so much as glance at him. His gaze remained on Charlotte, pinning her to her seat. "At Lady Whitmore's ball, I found you... intriguing. You spoke with candour when others simpered. You did not flinch when you ought to have. I have no desire for a wife who plays at affection, nor for the endless hunt of matchmaking mothers. You made plain what you offered, and I find myself, against better judgment, disposed to accept it. I do not require love. Only honesty. And in you, Lady Charlotte, I see that plainly enough."

Nicholas' eyes were blazing now. "This is madness. Charlotte—"

But Charlotte's heart, though beating wildly, felt curiously steady. This was what she had wanted: a title, security, freedom from whispers. This man was offering a union without risk of tenderness.

Her voice emerged clear, calm, without a tremor. "Yes, Your Grace. I accept."

Nicholas's head whipped toward her, still in utter disbelief of what he had just heard. "Charlotte!"

But the Duke of Duskbourne was already straightening, his expression as composed as if they had agreed upon a contract for land or trade. "Then it is settled." He bowed first to Nicholas, then to Charlotte. "You shall hear from me shortly."

And with that, he turned on his heel, striding from the parlour as abruptly as he had entered, leaving the echo of his presence behind like a draft through a door left ajar. Charlotte sat very still, her pulse thundering in her ears. She felt Nicholas's gaze upon her, hot with disbelief, protective fury, and something akin to betrayal.

The silence after the Duke's departure stretched long enough that Charlotte could hear the crackle of the fire in the grate as well as the ticking of the clock upon the mantel. Nicholas remained standing, staring at her as if she had grown a second head.

"Charlotte," he said at last in a voice that trembled at the edges. "Tell me you are not serious."

She could only nod once. "I am entirely serious, Nicholas."

Nicholas took a sharp breath and began to pace, with one hand raking through his dark hair. "A proposal in my very parlour! From a man you do not know! And you accept him without hesitation? For God's sake, Charlotte, are you certain of this?"

"Yes," she replied calmly, though her heart fluttered treacherously. "More certain than I have been of anything in my life."

He stopped before her, eyes searching her face for cracks. "This is Duskbourne we are speaking of. A man with a reputation for coldness, for shutting out the world. Do you think he will give you joy? Do you think he will make you happy?"

Charlotte drew in a breath, steady and sure. "Yes. Because happiness does not come from love, Nicholas. Not for me. It comes from security, from duty fulfilled, from freedom at last to live without the weight of whispers pressing upon me. He will not ask for my heart, and I will not ask for his. In that balance, I shall have peace."

Nicholas's expression softened, though anguish still shadowed his features. "Peace," he repeated, as though tasting the word. "But Charlotte, you deserve more than peace. You deserve joy, laughter, a husband who—"

She laid a gentle hand on his arm. "No," she said firmly. "I had joy once, Nicholas, and it ended in betrayal. No more dreams. No more folly. This is what I want."

He looked down at her, torn between outrage and love. Finally, with a ragged sigh, he cupped her hand in his.

"I would give you the world if I could, you know that," he murmured. "But if this is the path you swear will bring you happiness, I will not stand in your way."

Charlotte's throat tightened, but she forced a smile. "Thank you."

Nicholas pulled her into his arms, holding her close as he had when she was small and the world seemed too sharp. "Heavens help him if he does not honour you, Charlotte," he said fiercely. "For he will have me to answer to."

She closed her eyes against his shoulder, knowing she had won his blessing, though at the cost of his peace of mind. When Nicholas finally left her, muttering something about finding Lydia, the parlour felt too still and too wide. Charlotte crossed to the window and sank into the small chair tucked beside the drapery.

A book lay on the table. She picked it up, let it fall open at random, and tried to read. The words blurred almost at once, her eyes tracing lines but catching no meaning. Her thoughts returned again and again to the figure of Cassian Oberon, to his grey eyes, his voice like cut stone, and the brusque finality with which he had come and gone. Her future became sealed in a few curt sentences.

Suddenly, there was another knock on the door, and it startled her. Her maid stepped in after having been called, holding a sealed letter upon a tray.

"For you, my lady," she said softly.

Charlotte set her book aside and reached for it, but the sight of the familiar hand made her breath catch.

Edmund Larke.

Her stomach tightened. For a moment, she merely stared at the wax seal. She could feel the weight of it in her palm, as if she were holding a brick. One month ago, she would have clutched it to her breast and stolen away to her chamber to read it in secret. Then, she would feel herself seen, cherished, *adored*. Now, she felt nothing but the slow rise of anger.

"Leave me," she said quietly.

When the maid had gone, Charlotte stood up, moved to the fireplace, and without hesitation tossed the letter into the flames. The parchment curled at once, blackening, and the inked name dissolved into smoke. She watched until it was ash, until every trace of him was gone.

It was not sorrow she felt, nor even relief, but a strange, steady calm. The fantasy was over. Edmund Larke no longer had power over her.

Her past was ashes. As for her future, whether cold or safe or something else entirely, it now belonged to the Duke of Duskbourne.

Chapter Five

The scent of freshly dyed silks and pressed muslin hung in the air as Charlotte stepped into the high, sunlit room of Hawthorne Textiles the following day. Bolts of fabric, neatly stacked, gleamed in every shade from the softest cream to the deepest indigo. Seamstresses bent over their worktables, listening to the sound of the rhythmic whisper of shears and the steady clatter of needles.

Lydia moved among them with easy command, her fingers trailing lightly over the cloth as she gave instructions. It still amazed Charlotte, sometimes, to see her sister-in-law so firmly at the helm of this enterprise. What had once been a necessity had grown into a triumph: gowns and coats worn by half the ton, stitched under Lydia's eye.

"I shall need a wedding gown," Charlotte said, the words slipping into the busy air before she could second-guess them.

Lydia froze, turning so sharply that the seamstress beside her pricked her finger. "A what?"

Charlotte lifted her chin, keeping her expression carefully neutral. "A wedding gown. You are best placed to make it."

Lydia's eyes widened, then softened with dawning comprehension. She seized Charlotte's hands as her voice vibrated with excitement. "Charlotte, at last! You mean the poet? He has come for you? I knew he would."

The flush that rose to Charlotte's cheeks was sharp, unwelcome. She pulled her hands free. "Not the poet."

Lydia blinked. "Not the... then who?"

Charlotte straightened her gloves. "The Duke of Duskbourne."

For a moment, Lydia could only stare, her hazel eyes widening in astonishment. "Cassian Oberon?" she whispered. "He... he has proposed?"

"He has." Charlotte busied herself with a bolt of ivory silk, though her fingers lingered too long on the smooth weave. "And I have accepted."

"Goodness me," Lydia breathed, recovering herself enough to shoo the seamstress away for privacy. She leaned closer, her words tumbling out in a rush. "But how? When? The man never attends so much as a supper, and suddenly he appears, proposing marriage to you? Charlotte, you must tell me everything."

Charlotte smoothed the silk, her eyes fixed upon the pale shimmer of the fabric. "There is little to tell. He has need of a wife. I have need of a husband. The arrangement suits us both."

"That is not *little to tell*," Lydia insisted, but now her astonishment was softening into concern. "Charlotte, is this what you truly want?"

Charlotte forced herself to meet her sister-in-law's gaze, just like she had her brother's. "It is precisely what I want."

Lydia studied her for a long moment, clearly unconvinced but unwilling to press further. At last, she sighed, brushing a stray curl from her brow. "Very well. But if I am to design your gown, do not imagine I shall make it plain or dull, no matter how sensible you sound. A Montclair wedding deserves silk worthy of the name."

Lydia's astonishment then gave way to something far brighter: excitement. She clapped her hands together, already assessing bolts of fabric as though they were soldiers ready to be commanded.

"Oh, Charlotte, I shall make you radiant," Lydia declared, her eyes flashing. "You shall glow so brilliantly, the ton will have no choice but to hush their gossip and admire you. Ivory, certainly, perhaps trimmed with silver thread, or pearls along the hem... yes, pearls will catch the candlelight beautifully. And a veil, of course, though you have the profile for a tiara..."

Charlotte let Lydia's words wash over her. It was a tide of enthusiasm she could not quite step into. She traced a finger along the edge of a bolt of satin, smooth and flawless beneath her touch, but felt nothing stir in her chest.

Once, she might have dreamt of this, of the perfect gown, of a husband whose eyes lit with devotion as she walked toward him. But now the thought only tightened something in her ribs. This wedding was not a dream. It was an arrangement. It was an agreement made in measured words, without affection, without tenderness.

What did it matter what gown she wore?

Still, she forced a small smile for Lydia's sake. "You will design whatever you think best. I do not mind the particulars."

Lydia's hands stilled at the words, her brows drawing together as she turned back to Charlotte. "Do not mind? Charlotte, my dear, this is your wedding."

Charlotte smiled. "It is a wedding, yes. But not the sort that requires fuss. I am not marrying for gowns or for admiration."

Lydia squeezed both Charlotte's hands. "Then I shall make certain your gown speaks for you, even if you will not. You shall stand at the altar not as a spinster, not as a shadow, but as a duchess. And I swear, Charlotte, you will glow."

Charlotte swallowed against the ache in her throat, returning Lydia's smile with practiced serenity.

Glow, yes. Even if the light is not my own.

***

"You devil," Gideon exclaimed as he burst through the door of Cassian's study, with a rolled newspaper clutched in his hand. He strode across the carpet and let it fall with a dramatic slap upon his friend's writing table. "I must find out like *this* that your marriage is a done deal?"

Cassian looked up from his correspondence, his expression cool, unruffled. "You knew it was already arranged. I merely went there to confirm."

Gideon dropped into the opposite chair with all the grace of a man who had never taken anything seriously in his life.

"Cassian, the ton is already in hysterics. Lady Charlotte Montclair, risen from the ashes of spinsterhood to become your duchess? They are all fainting into their teacups. And you..." He gestured with a careless wave. "You sit here as though it were no more significant than adjusting the price of barley."

Cassian returned to his letter, unmoved. "It is precisely as I told you: a practical arrangement. There is nothing more to say."

"Nothing more to say?" Gideon repeated, his grin widening. "You vanish into a retiring room with the lady, reappear with her proposal still echoing in your ears, and within a fortnight the banns will be read. Forgive me, Cassian, but that is *something* to say."

Cassian's mouth curved in the faintest suggestion of a smile, although dry and humourless. "I imagine you will continue to say it, regardless of my silence."

"Of course I will," Gideon said cheerfully, sprawling back in his chair. "For I cannot decide what astonishes me more: that

41

she dared propose it, or that you actually accepted. I must say, I thought you were telling me you would speak to her just so I would stop pestering you about it."

Cassian shrugged indifferently. "It is all as you yourself presented it: sensible."

Gideon chuckled, shaking his head. "Sensible, perhaps. But I have known you too long, Cassian. For all your iron logic, something about Lady Charlotte unsettled you. I saw it in your face the night you told me. Admit it."

Cassian's gaze hardened, but he said nothing. He would not admit aloud that her fire, her defiance, and her unflinching calm had struck him like no woman's gaze had since Eleanor.

Gideon leaned forward. "You see? Even your silence betrays you. I think you may find this *convenience* far less convenient than you think."

He then snatched the paper back up and shook it at him. "And do you know this is *all* they are writing about? Columns upon columns of speculation. Half of them paint Lady Charlotte as a tragic recluse, the other half as some mysterious enchantress who has bewitched the Duke of Duskbourne. Your name is inked across every page, Cassian. Every teapot in Mayfair will be rattling over it before luncheon."

Cassian steepled his fingers, his expression as cool and unreadable as stone. "And I care not in the least."

"Oh, come now," Gideon said with a laugh, dropping the paper again. "Not even a flicker of irritation?"

Cassian's mouth thinned. "Only that it will encourage every bore in London to seek me out. They will want to speak of it, to ask their idiotic questions, to offer their tedious congratulations. That, Gideon, I despise."

Gideon leaned back in his chair, grinning like a schoolboy who had caught out his tutor. "Ah, there it is, that spark of feeling I was looking for. Not about the lady, mind you, but rather about your hatred for conversation."

Cassian shot him a look of long-suffering patience. "Must you always be insufferable?"

"It is my life's purpose," Gideon replied promptly. "And it is my particular joy when the great Duke of Duskbourne lowers himself to admit that society vexes him."

Despite himself, Cassian let out a soft breath that might have been a laugh. Gideon's teasing was relentless, but there was no malice in it, only the easy familiarity of a friendship weathered by years, battles in Parliament, and confidences never repeated.

"You may enjoy my suffering too much," Cassian said dryly.

"Undoubtedly," Gideon agreed. "But you must admit, Cassian, that this business of matrimony has made you far more interesting company than you have been in years."

Cassian shook his head in exasperation, though the corner of his mouth betrayed the faintest upward curve. "You are impossible."

"And yet," Gideon said with a rakish grin, "you keep me."

Cassian looked at him, while his grey eyes softened ever so slightly. "That, Gideon, is the one thing I will not call absurd." He reached for the stack of estate ledgers on his desk, drawing them closer with deliberate precision. "Now be gone with your follies. I have actual work to do, something a man like you would not understand."

Gideon barked a laugh, rising easily from his chair. "Work? Yes, Cassian, drown yourself in your beloved numbers and harvest reports. I shall leave you to them, since you find them more tolerable company than your oldest friend."

He circled the desk, clapped Cassian soundly on the shoulder, and added with infuriating cheer, "But do not think I'll cease teasing you. Oh no, my friend. I'll be toasting your marriage of convenience in every club from White's to Boodle's before the week is out."

Cassian gave him a level look. "Try, and you'll find yourself without brandy in your glass for a month."

Gideon only grinned wider, tipped an imaginary hat, and sauntered out, leaving the faint scent of tobacco and amusement in his wake. The door shut, and silence reclaimed the study.

Cassian set his jaw and returned to the ledger before him, though the words blurred. He sat back in his chair and allowed his gaze to drift to the fire.

Marriage.

The word settled heavily upon him, as though spoken aloud, it might alter the very air. Yet what would truly change? A wife in name, a duchess at Duskbourne. There would be appearances to maintain, duties to fulfil. But his solitude, which had now become the core of his existence, needed not be disturbed. Lady Charlotte had made it clear she wanted nothing of him but title and protection. He, in turn, had no intention of offering more.

Yes. Little would change.

He convinced himself of it as one convinces oneself of a necessary truth: by repetition and by cold reason. *A marriage of convenience, without affection, without risk.*

And yet, unbidden, the memory of her bright, fierce eyes rose before him, as vivid as the crackling firelight. Cassian exhaled slowly, as if to banish the image.

Little would change, he reminded himself again.

Chapter Six

The bells tolled in a sound that was both solemn and sweet, but they might as well have been for another bride.

Charlotte was standing at the altar, with her hand resting in the Duke's. Her gaze was fixed on the clergyman as the ceremony wound its stately course. She smiled when required, spoke when prompted, and lowered her lashes with quiet decorum. Her every gesture was faultless, her every word correct.

And all the while, she felt nothing.

This day should have meant *something*. It should have carried the weight of a heart laid bare, trembling joy, tears perhaps, vows spoken with conviction. She had once dreamt of such a day in girlish foolishness. She had pictured lace and flowers, candlelight and a kiss that promised forever.

But those dreams were long buried.

Now she performed the motions as if rehearsed. The ivory gown Lydia had designed shimmered beautifully in the candlelight, and her veil floated like mist. Her voice was soft and steady as she spoke the words every bride spoke.

She did not falter. She did not blush. She did not tremble.

And that, she thought with a pang, was exactly wrong.

Beside her, the Duke was carved from the same composure. His hand was firm, and his voice was resonant as he delivered his vows without hesitation and without warmth. He was every inch a duke, solemn and unyielding, a man who had bound himself to duty long before binding himself to her.

They fit the picture perfectly: a flawless match.

"The Lord make His face to shine upon you and be gracious unto you." The clergyman's voice rose solemnly through the vaulted chapel, echoing against stone and stained glass.

The Duke's hand enclosed hers.

"I now pronounce you man and wife."

The words seemed to hang in the air, final and irrevocable. Charlotte drew a breath and lifted her gaze. The Duke's eyes met hers.

"Duchess," he said softly, with the faintest inclination of his head.

It was not endearment, nor triumph. It was merely a fact stated and a title bestowed.

Her lips curved into the smallest smile, for she had to show the picture of a happy bride. "Your Grace."

For a moment, nothing more passed between them. There was no whispered promise and no tender clasp of fingers. The silence itself felt like an unspoken vow. Around them, the congregation stirred with polite applause, erupting into a rustle of fans and murmured well-wishes. Nicholas's eyes revealed restrained concern, while Lydia dabbed discreetly at her eyes with a handkerchief.

Charlotte lowered her lashes as she let her hand rest lightly against the Duke's arm. Then, she whispered the only words that came to her lips. "It is done."

The Duke's reply was low and without any inflection. "It is."

The bells had scarcely ceased their tolling when the onslaught began.

"Congratulations, Your Grace," murmured one gentleman with an elaborate bow, his wife pressing forward to curtsy with equal eagerness. "A most fortunate match."

"Astonishingly fortunate," added another, as her fan fluttered too fast and her eyes darted toward Charlotte's gown as if measuring its worth.

Charlotte inclined her head, and her lips curved in a polite smile that felt carved from porcelain. She accepted their words, their touches on her sleeve, their shallow praise, all the while acutely aware of the glances exchanged just beyond her notice.

The whispers slithered like snakes through the air, never loud enough to confront but always sharp enough to pierce. Charlotte held her spine straight. Her arm rested lightly upon the Duke's as if it were the most natural thing in the world.

If *he* heard the murmurs, he gave no sign. His expression remained composed, and his answers were clipped and courteous. As they walked back down the aisle, he accepted congratulations with the same gravitas he would have lent to a speech in Parliament: neither warmer nor colder than necessity required.

Charlotte, meanwhile, forced her smile to hold. Each curtsy and each simpering remark tested the edges of her resolve. Her cheeks burned with the weight of every speculative glance, every whispered comparison to what she had been, to what she was now.

And yet, she did not falter.

One lady, emboldened by her companions, spoke with malice that was too sweet. "How very extraordinary, Your Grace, that you should capture the heart of Duskbourne."

"Extraordinary, indeed," Charlotte offered as response. "And precisely as it should be."

The lady faltered, but Charlotte moved past her without pause.

Let them whisper, she thought, while her hand tightened ever so slightly upon the Duke's arm. *Let them doubt, let them pry. They will not see me bend.*

Then, Nicholas and Lydia threaded their way through the press of well-wishers.

"Charlotte," Nicholas said, his voice gentler than his expression. He bent to kiss her cheek, lingering a fraction longer than custom demanded. "Congratulations, dearest sister."

"Indeed," Lydia added quickly. Her smile was warm, but her eyes were sharp as they flicked toward the Duke. "We wish you every happiness, both of you."

The Duke inclined his head, his manner as composed as ever. "Your good wishes are received with thanks. And you are, of course, welcome at Duskbourne in due course... once my duchess and I are properly settled."

The words were perfectly correct, yet they carried the finality of a line drawn. Nicholas's jaw tightened, though he returned the bow with dignified restraint.

Lydia, who was never one to let silence linger, clasped Charlotte's hands briefly. "I am so sorry there will be no wedding breakfast. It feels... unusual, and I had hoped to celebrate you properly."

"Yes," the Duke said at once. "We preferred it thus."

Charlotte forced her lips into a serene smile, though her chest felt tight, but she did not meet her sister-in-law's gaze. She could not bear to.

After they had said their goodbyes, Charlotte and the Duke headed for the waiting carriage. When Duskbourne helped her inside, his touch was brief and formal.

The door closed with a decisive thud. Then, the horses jolted into motion, the wheels crunched against gravel, and London began to recede behind them.

Inside, the silence was oppressive. The velvet interior seemed too small for the space between them. The Duke sat opposite her, impeccably still, his grey eyes fixed upon the window. Charlotte folded her hands in her lap, smoothing the skirts Lydia had so lovingly arranged. She opened her mouth once, searching for words, but found none. After all, what did one say to a husband who was little more than a stranger?

"Comfortable enough?" The Duke asked at last. Charlotte knew it was the kind of courtesy that demanded no real answer, but she spoke anyway.

"Yes," she said softly. Nothing more.

The silence returned, thick as fog. The steady rhythm of the horses' hooves seemed to grow louder, and the sway of the carriage was now more pronounced. Charlotte kept her gaze lowered, aware of every breath and every heartbeat.

She longed, absurdly, to ask him what he thought of her gown, whether he regretted his decision already, whether he had felt the same hollow ache when speaking his vows. But her pride held her tongue still.

Better silence than foolishness.

***

The carriage ride to Kent was only a few hours, but in the silence of the carriage, it seemed to last an eternity. Then finally, Charlotte drew back the curtain and caught her first glimpse of Duskbourne Hall.

It rose from the fields like some vast, brooding sentinel, with its dark stone walls against a pewter sky and its countless windows glimmering faintly in the dim light. Turrets loomed at the corners, while ivy clung to the façades like veins. It was not a house built to charm, but to endure and to command.

Charlotte's breath caught. It was magnificent, yes, but in that stark, gothic way that seemed almost too vast for human habitation. Already she felt herself small before it.

The carriage rolled to a halt before the great steps. Outside, the servants had arranged themselves in two straight lines, stretching from the gravel sweep to the front doors. They stood in precise ranks in complete silence, wearing immaculate uniforms. However, their gazes were lowered as though awaiting inspection from a master who was bound to find something wrong.

The Duke stepped out of the carriage first. Even without words, his presence filled the space, while order and discipline seemed to ripple outward from him. He turned, extended a gloved hand, and helped her descend. Charlotte placed her fingers lightly in his, acutely aware of the many eyes upon her. The Duke released her hand once she stood beside him.

His voice, when he spoke, carried easily across the neat rows.

"My household," he said. "This is your new mistress, the Duchess of Duskbourne."

A ripple passed through the assembly, though no one moved. Each servant dipped in unison, whether it was a bow or a curtsy, like soldiers executing a drill. Charlotte managed a polite smile, though the weight of their collective silence pressed heavily upon her. It was not welcome, she felt, but scrutiny. Dozens of eyes were watching her, measuring her, even if none dared lift their gaze.

She inclined her head, forcing her voice into a steadiness she did not feel. "I am pleased to be here. I trust we shall serve each other well."

The Duke's grey eyes flicked briefly toward her before he turned and led the way up the steps. The vast doors swung open as they approached, revealing a cavernous hall beyond entirely made up of dark wood, high ceilings, and the faint chill of stone that had never quite lost the moorland damp.

The echo of their footsteps followed them into the great hall. It was large, with dark panelled walls and a vaulted ceiling from which iron chandeliers hung like cages. A sweeping staircase rose before them. Its polished banister was gleaming impeccably, but the Duke did not pause to admire it.

"Duskbourne is efficient," he announced, as though reading from a ledger rather than presenting his home. "You will find everything in its proper place. Order here is paramount."

Charlotte nodded, her gaze sweeping over the carved oak doors that lined the hall, each one leading into a chamber that could have swallowed her childhood home whole.

He led her first into the drawing room, which was vast but austere, untouched by the frivolity of fashionable silks or gilt. Then the library, with its shelves rising floor-to-ceiling, filled with neat ranks of books. The air there smelled faintly of leather and ink, and though the Duke did not linger, Charlotte caught the trace of reverence in the way his hand brushed the spine of a volume as he passed.

"The dining room," he continued, indicating another double door that remained closed. "The music room is seldom used. The chapel you may see later if you wish."

They moved through corridors that seemed to stretch endlessly, past portraits of dukes long dead, but whose eyes were still very much alive and watchful. Charlotte's slippers whispered against the stone. She was overwhelmed by the knowledge that she had stepped into a house ruled not by warmth but by memory and order.

At last, the Duke gestured down a long passage where the air seemed to grow colder and the shadows thicker. The doors here were shuttered, and the sconces around it unlit.

"This wing is closed," he said flatly. "It has remained so for many years. You will not enter."

Charlotte turned toward him, with questions rising to her lips, but his expression allowed for none. His grey eyes remained shuttered as tightly as the doors.

She inclined her head. "As you wish."

They walked on, while her curiosity burned like a flame she dared not feed. Once the tour had reached its end, Charlotte knew one thing for sure: the Duke of Duskbourne's house was a fortress, and like its master, it kept its secrets well.

Chapter Seven

"Sit," the Duke said, gesturing toward the leather chair opposite his writing table.

Charlotte lowered herself onto the seat, glancing around. His study was much as she had imagined it: shelves of law books, neat stacks of correspondence, ledgers aligned in perfect order. This was a room of business, not comfort.

Her husband settled into his own chair, his long frame seeming to fill the space. He regarded her with that cool, steady gaze she was beginning to understand was as much armour as his black coat.

"We should be clear on the practical arrangements," he began. His tone was measured. "You will find the household accounts in order. The running of Duskbourne's domestic wing is now your responsibility. Mrs. Redfern, the housekeeper, will answer to you. As for the estates, I will continue to oversee their management."

Charlotte folded her hands in her lap. "Of course."

"You will not be expected to attend many social events," he continued, "though there will be occasions when your presence in London is required. At such times, appearances will matter. You will conduct yourself as a duchess, which means you shall be polite, gracious, and beyond reproach. You are not to encourage gossip."

Her lips curved in a faint, practiced smile. "I believe I have had enough gossip to last a lifetime, Your Grace. I intend to provide no fuel for further fire."

For the first time, the corner of his mouth shifted, which was as close to amusement as she had yet seen in him. "Good. Then we understand each other."

"And what of... expectations between us?" she asked, feeling as if her own voice would betray her. "Are we to..." She felt an onslaught of heat in her cheeks, but she had to clarify her question. "Are we to be intimate with each other?"

The Duke's grey and unblinking eyes lifted to hers. He regarded her a moment, as though weighing his words, then spoke with cool precision. "That, my lady, is your choice. If you wish it, it shall be so. If not, then it will not be forced upon you. I do not find you unattractive," he added, "so it would not be a hardship on my part."

The detached way he said it, in such a manner that was stripped of intimacy, of warmth, of even the faintest tenderness, made Charlotte's throat tighten. He spoke as though he were discussing rent rolls or crop yields.

She lowered her gaze, unable to stop her hands from twisting together in her lap. "I see," she murmured. A pause stretched, and the fire snapped in the hearth as if to remind her that a response was needed. "Then I shall... think about it."

"Very well," the Duke replied simply. "In that case, that would be all. You may go and find one of the maids. They will show you to your chambers."

With those words, he returned his attention to the stack of correspondence at his elbow, as though the subject were settled. Charlotte sat a moment longer, feeling the weight of his words pressing upon her chest. She had thought she wanted this practicality, duty, a union untroubled by passion. Yet something in his cool dismissal unsettled her and left her feeling oddly hollow where she had expected only relief.

At last, she rose, curtsying slightly. "Thank you, Your Grace."

He merely nodded, then his attention was focused on the papers before him. And with that, Charlotte withdrew into the shadows of the great hall, with her heart feeling heavier than ever. She made her way down the corridor slowly, lost in thought. In fact, she was so focused that a voice startled her when it addressed her.

"Your Grace?"

A young woman stepped forward with a curtsy. Her manner was respectful yet not timid. "I am Miriam, your maid. His Grace assigned me to you especially. If you will follow me, I will show you to your chambers."

Charlotte inclined her head, grateful for the interruption to her uneasy reflections. "Thank you, Miriam."

The maid led her up the sweeping staircase and down another hall where sconces burned more warmly. At the end of the passage, Miriam opened a pair of doors with a discreet flourish. Charlotte drew in a breath.

The chamber before her was lovely; so lovely in fact, that for a moment she could not move. Tall windows looked out across the moors, nestled between curtains of heavy silk in muted shades of blue and silver. A grand bed stood at the centre, its carved posts draped with sheer muslin that glimmered faintly in the lamplight. The hearth already burned with a welcoming fire, and a writing desk near the window gleamed with polished wood. A stack of fresh paper was already waiting upon it.

It was not austere, nor as cold as the rest of the house. This room had been prepared with care, even thoughtfulness. Strange though it might have been, it was meant for her.

Charlotte turned to Miriam, who was watching her with quiet expectation. "It is... beautiful," she said softly, her voice catching despite herself. "Thank you."

Miriam smiled faintly. "His Grace ordered it specially for you, my lady. Everything was chosen and readied these past weeks."

Charlotte blinked, surprised. Cassian Oberon, who spoke of their marriage like a contract, had ensured this chamber was made ready. Not only ready, but lovely and welcoming.

"I see," Charlotte murmured, lowering her gaze so Miriam would not read too much in her expression.

Miriam bobbed another curtsy. "If you should require anything, you have only to ring."

"Thank you," Charlotte said again, more warmly this time.

When Miriam departed, Charlotte walked slowly across the chamber. Her fingers trailed over the embroidered coverlet, the polished writing desk, the silken curtains. She sank onto the edge of the bed, staring into the fire.

So this was her new life as the Duchess of Duskbourne, with rooms prepared in her honour and with a house that breathed order and silence around her.

She folded her hands in her lap, whispering to herself as much as to the firelight. "Then I must learn how to belong here."

And with that, Charlotte Montclair... no, Charlotte Oberon now, began to settle into the unfamiliar role she had chosen, with her heart still uncertain, but her will unbending.

***

"For the love of everything holy, Cassian, tell me I am not seeing this right."

Cassian looked up from the glass of brandy he had scarcely touched. Gideon lounged across from him at White's, with a wicked gleam in his eye and his tone dripping with incredulity.

"You were married this morning," Gideon went on, waving a hand as though to sweep aside all possible excuses, "and yet here you sit at White's today, glowering into your drink like some monk at confession. Why, pray, are you not at Duskbourne Hall, warming your wife's bed?"

Cassian's expression did not flicker. He took a measured sip of brandy, then set the glass down with deliberate calm. "Because the estate requires attention."

Gideon barked a laugh. "The estate! Oh, that is rich. I should have known. Marriage to the Duke of Duskbourne: vows at noon, ledgers by dawn. And I'm guessing, you are here for a brief respite."

Cassian's jaw tightened, though his voice remained even. "Do not jest, Gideon. The tenants require fair rents before winter. The harvest was short in two villages to the north. I have already sent instructions for supplemental grain stores. If I do not keep order, who will?"

"You are insufferable," Gideon said cheerfully, leaning back in his chair. "Here I sit, expecting scandal, intrigue, perhaps even a blush or two, and instead you give me crop yields."

Cassian's grey eyes flicked toward him sharply. "It is better than indulgent folly."

"Indulgent folly is precisely the point of marriage, Cassian," Gideon retorted with a smirk. "At least in its first nights. Tell me, did the poor lady weep when you left her to her embroidery and fled to your beloved club?"

Cassian exhaled through his nose slowly, as though restraining himself from snapping the stem of his glass. "You assume too much."

"Then enlighten me," Gideon pressed like an impatient child. "Do you mean to tell me you've a beautiful new duchess waiting in your halls, and you spend your evening among smoke and brandy with me?"

Cassian shifted uneasily. "My marriage is as it was agreed: an arrangement of convenience. There is no need for... expectations."

"Convenience," Gideon repeated, savouring the word like fine wine. He leaned forward, lowering his voice. "Then why do you look as though you've not slept a moment in two days?"

Cassian's silence was answer enough. He reached for the newspaper beside him, unfolding it with precision. "We have wasted enough breath. What I came here to discuss are matters of shipping. The wool contracts—"

Gideon groaned, throwing his head back. "You truly are hopeless. Here I try to coax a confession, and instead you bury me beneath wool and accounts. Fine, then, tell me about the damned contracts. But do not think I will cease reminding you: you are married, Cassian. And sooner or later, you must start living as though you are."

Cassian's lips thinned, but he turned the page of his notes with unruffled calm.

"Then let us begin with the shipments," he said.

Chapter Eight

The hour was very late when Cassian returned to Duskbourne.

The great house loomed out of the fog, with its windows glinting faintly like watchful eyes. Inside, the corridors stretched long and hollow, lit only by the occasional sconce sputtering against the dark. Silence pressed close on every side, broken now and then by the low hiss of dying embers in the hearths, as though the house itself exhaled in weary sighs.

Cassian moved with the ease of habit, the hallways as familiar to him as the weight of grief in his chest. Yet tonight, something broke the stillness. He noticed a figure. A woman stood a little way ahead, caught in the lamplight like a wraith.

It could only be *her.*

Her hair spilled loose about her shoulders, pale as the muslin nightgown that clung to her form. Her bare feet shifted on the stone floor as she turned uncertainly toward one of the doors, then paused, her face marked with confusion and faint dismay.

For an instant, Cassian halted. The sight of her so unguarded and vulnerable, yet luminous against the gloom, struck him with unwelcome force. His gaze swept her figure before discipline snapped him back into himself, and he became cold and controlled once more.

"Lost, Duchess?" His voice was low, although the silence made it sound louder than he intended.

His question startled her, and she turned to him. "I... I could not find my chamber. The corridors look the same at night."

He stepped forward, and his shadow stretched long against the wall. "Duskbourne is a labyrinth. You should have called for your maid."

"I did not wish to disturb her," she murmured.

"Come," he said, heading in the direction of the darkest corridor. "I will see you back."

They walked in silence as the house loomed around them with its watchful portraits and endless doors. He refused to admit it, even to himself, but her presence unsettled him. He was maddeningly aware of her nearness, her scent of lavender, and the sound of her bare feet whispering against the stone. He kept his eyes forward, steadily willing himself not to notice what he already had.

After some moments, Charlotte's voice broke the hush. "This house is... vast. Almost endless. I see why I lost my way."

He inclined his head faintly. "Duskbourne was built to endure, not to comfort. In time, you will learn its turns."

Her gaze drifted down a branching corridor, darker than the rest. It was the shuttered wing. Cassian felt her attention shift even before she spoke.

"And that way?" she asked quietly. "The wing you mentioned earlier... the one that is closed?"

He stopped. The weight of her question hung heavy in the air between them. Slowly, he turned his head toward her.

"Do not ask about it." His voice was sharper now, stripped of courtesy, carrying a finality that echoed against the stone. "That part of the house is closed, and it will remain so. You are not to enter. *Ever.*"

For a moment, he thought that he might have spoken to her too harshly. After all, she had only asked out of innocent curiosity, unable to know what had happened and completely oblivious to the terrible secret that he had to live with. But it was a burden he would carry alone.

Charlotte's lips parted as though she might press him further, but something in his expression must have silenced her. She looked away, then continued following him.

He somehow knew she would not remain quiet for the remainder of their walk. So, he was not surprised when she murmured, "There is something I must tell you, Your Grace. I intend to continue my charitable work here. The orphanages, the pensions for widows, the poorhouse..." She drew a breath as if to steady herself. "They are not duties I will relinquish."

Cassian's gaze remained fixed forward, his stride never faltering. "Very well. You may continue. But you will do so with proper protection. A chaperone will attend to you whenever you leave Duskbourne."

She halted upon his words. Her eyes flashed up at him, not waiting for him to stop as well. "That is unnecessary. I have managed perfectly well on my own thus far. My brother always allowed me the freedom to go alone, and I intend to keep it."

His jaw tightened, and the coldness in his voice surprised even him. "I am not your brother."

Once again, he felt as if he had been too harsh. Years of solitary confinement could easily do that to a man. And now, he had to relearn how to actually speak to another human being. It was all bothersome.

Still, it was difficult to be patient with her when all his instincts were crying out that he had to protect her from whatever dangers lurked in the shadows. *I will protect this wife, even if I could not protect my first.*

Charlotte's blue eyes glared at him defiantly despite the flush on her cheeks. "No, you are not. But I am not a child to be herded about. I will not have every errand shadowed as though I cannot be trusted."

"It is not a matter of trust. You are not to be left vulnerable," Cassian returned. His every word was controlled but edged with steel. "You carry my name now. What befalls you reflects upon me. I will not have my duchess wandering the streets unprotected."

Silence coiled, thick and taut as wire. Neither yielded, and neither softened. For a heartbeat, Cassian found himself staring at her, struck by the fire in her gaze and that unflinching resolve. An unwelcome part of him admired it, even as it infuriated him.

At last, he turned, resuming their stride with clipped precision. They reached her chamber door in silence. He bowed before her curtly, barely even looking at her.

"Good night, Duchess."

Her answer came as coolly. "Good night, Your Grace."

Cassian walked the length of the corridor with the deliberate stride of a man who must keep moving or else feel too much. Charlotte's voice still echoed in his mind, alive with the same stubborn fire that both drew and defied him. He reached his study, closed the door behind him, and let the silence rush back in.

The fire had burned low. Only embers remained, pulsing faintly in the grate like the last breath of something dying. He crossed to the sideboard, uncorked the decanter, and poured himself a generous measure of brandy. There was no ceremony, just the dull sound of liquid striking glass.

He drank it in one swallow. The burn in his throat was sharp, almost welcome. He poured another, slower this time, staring into the amber depths as if they might hold answers. But of course, there were none.

The house was vast, but it felt small now. It was too close and too alive with her presence. He could still see Charlotte as she had stood in the corridor, pale in the half-light, unbowed beneath his sharp words. The scent of lavender still lingered faintly in the air.

Cassian turned from the fire, crossing to the far corner of the room where an old cabinet stood locked. It was a piece no servant touched. He withdrew a small key from his waistcoat pocket, fitted it to the lock, and opened the top drawer.

Inside, wrapped in worn linen, lay a portrait. He lifted it carefully, as one might lift something breakable or sacred.

Eleanor.

Her face smiled up at him from the painted oval. Her brown eyes were bright, and her beautiful lips curved in that familiar, effortless warmth that could still hollow him out from the inside. She had been painted in the garden at Duskbourne, with the sunlight glinting through her hair.

He remembered that day. The painter had been rather slow, even for a nervous man, and Eleanor had teased him for making her sit so long. She had worn a pale green gown and had plucked a sprig of rosemary from the garden hedge, holding it to her nose as she smiled.

"For remembrance," she had said, while her eyes sparkled like stars.

A cruel jest now.

He swallowed hard, feeling the memory cut sharper than the brandy in his throat. He could almost hear her laugh echoing faintly through the study. It was that same laugh that had once filled every hall of Duskbourne, chasing the shadows from its corners.

He had killed that laughter.

He sank into his chair, holding the portrait cradled in his hands.

"Forgive me," he murmured, the words escaping before he could stop them. His voice was so low that they barely made a sound at all. "I told myself I would never…"

But the sentence faltered. His throat closed around the rest. The brandy on his tongue turned bitter. He set the glass aside and brushed his thumb lightly over the painted cheek as if touch might bridge the years between them.

"You deserved more than this," he said quietly. "More than me. I could not save you. And now…"

His voice broke. He exhaled in a long and hollow sound, but it was swallowed by the crackle of the fire.

After a moment, he placed the portrait back in its wrapping and returned it to its drawer, locking it away again as carefully as before. When he straightened, his face was once more the mask of the Duke of Duskbourne: controlled, composed, untouched.

But as he turned toward the dying fire, he felt its faint warmth against his skin and thought, for one unbearable instant, of Charlotte's eyes in the dark. He drank again, deeper this time, wishing for the silence of Duskbourne to swallow him whole.

Chapter Nine

"I am quite capable of managing on my own, Miriam."

Charlotte's words were spoken gently, though a trace of frustration coloured them as she adjusted her bonnet before the looking glass.

"Yes, Your Grace," the maid replied mildly. "His Grace instructed that I am to accompany you whenever you go in the village."

Charlotte met the girl's reflection. It was earnest, deferential, and far too young to have become the symbol of her husband's control. She sighed.

"Then I suppose I must endure it. Come along, Miriam. The hungry will not wait upon the Duke's permission."

The maid seemed satisfied as she dipped into a small curtsey. "Yes, Your Grace."

It was a bright but brittle morning, with the sunlight cutting across the fields in thin blades that failed to warm the air. The carriage rattled down the long road toward the village, and Charlotte sat in silence, watching the bleak sweep of land roll past. Duskbourne Hall loomed behind them like a shadow that refused to lift.

When they reached the parish church, the familiar rhythm of charitable work began, but it felt different now. The air inside the church was thick with the scent of stew and wood smoke, with the faint hum of voices as villagers gathered for their midday meal. Charlotte removed her gloves, set them aside, and began directing the preparations as she always had.

"Mrs. Pritchard, take these loaves to the children's table, if you please," she said. "And see that the broth is shared fairly, we don't want anyone left wanting."

The widow smiled gratefully, taking the bread. "Aye, Your Grace."

The title struck her like a foreign word. It still felt borrowed, ill-fitting, as though it belonged to some other woman entirely.

She worked steadily, ladling soup, speaking with the tenants and widows who came to thank her, but the ease she had once known was gone. Before, she had come here as Charlotte Montclair, who was unobserved and known simply for her kindness. Now every word was weighed and every glance deferential. The townsfolk bowed and murmured *Your Grace*, while their gratitude was tempered by awe, or perhaps caution.

And Miriam stood near the doorway, as a constant reminder of her husband's command. The girl's presence was discreet but suffocating all the same.

Charlotte offered a reassuring smile to a mother with a babe in her arms, her heart twisting as she did. The same work, the same people, and yet everything had changed. The invisible thread of freedom that had once bound her to this place had been cut, replaced by the silken cords of duty.

When the crowd thinned, she leaned lightly against one of the church pews, wiping her hands with a cloth. The sound of children laughing echoed faintly through the open door, and she felt it then, that hollow ache of a life that was no longer quite her own.

A few hours later, Miriam approached her. "Shall I fetch the carriage, Your Grace?"

Charlotte nodded, forcing her composure into place. "Yes, Miriam. It's time we returned to Duskbourne."

As Miriam stepped away to summon the carriage, Charlotte moved toward the church gate. Her gaze drifted across the square, and then her breath caught. There, beside the apothecary's shop, stood a figure she had not expected to see.

Edmund Larke.

He was speaking with another man, gesturing animatedly, and he had that same affected smile curving his lips that he'd worn the day she'd last seen him. He looked unchanged, save for the faint shadow of stubble and the easy, careless grace that had first fooled her.

The world seemed to tilt for a moment.

He had told her, once, that he was forever traveling to Bath, to London, to the Lakes, that the life of a poet was restless, rootless, haunted by inspiration. And yet here he was, standing in the same village square she had known all her life.

He never left at all.

Charlotte's gloved hand tightened around the iron gate. A tremor of humiliation coursed through her. It was not the sharp, fresh sting of betrayal, but something duller and deeper. She recognized it immediately as grief for her own foolishness.

She could not imagine now that she had ever believed a word that he told her, that she had once poured her heart into words for him, words she had never spoken aloud to anyone else. She had built a dream upon lies by offering her trust to a man who never deserved it.

How had she ever thought she loved him?

Her chest tightened, though the pain was quieter than it had once been. Now, after some time had passed, it was less the cut of a wound, and more the ache of an old scar. She realized, with a shiver, that he had never truly known her either. To him, she had been a name, a purse, a foolish woman who mistook his counterfeit verses for love.

Edmund laughed at something his companion said. The sound drifted faintly across the square, a ghost of a voice she had once longed to hear.

He did not see her.

And yet Charlotte could not help but wonder… Did he know? Did he read the announcements, see her name in print beside the Duke of Duskbourne's? Did he wonder why his letters had gone unanswered, why the woman he had planned to deceive had vanished so completely?

Her pulse quickened, as unease prickled at the back of her neck. She turned sharply as Miriam approached.

"Your Grace?" the maid asked quietly, following her gaze. "Is something amiss?"

"No," Charlotte said at once, gathering herself. "It's nothing at all. Come, Miriam. We should return."

She stepped into the waiting carriage without looking back. But as the horses started forward, she could not shake the image of Edmund standing there in the pale morning light, so ordinary and so small.

Once, he had shattered her world. Now he was merely a man in a grey coat on a street she no longer belonged to. And that, she realized with quiet certainty, was its own kind of freedom.

The road back to Duskbourne wound through the lush fields. Inside the carriage, the air felt stifling. Charlotte sat rigidly with her gloved hands folded in her lap, but her mind would not still. She turned toward Miriam, who sat across from her, with her eyes focused on the window.

"Tell me, Miriam," Charlotte said after a long silence, needing to fill the silent void with something. "How long have you served His Grace?"

The maid blinked, obviously surprised by the question. "Three years, Your Grace."

"And... he is a good master?"

Miriam hesitated a fraction too long. "Yes, Your Grace. The Duke is fair."

Charlotte arched a brow. "Fair? That is all?"

The maid's gaze flickered to her hands. "His Grace is particular about his household. He expects things done properly. But he is not unkind."

It was the sort of answer that told her more than it said.

Charlotte looked out the window again, watching the moors blur before focusing on her reflection in the glass. "Does he spend time with his staff? Or with anyone, for that matter?"

"No, Your Grace," Miriam said quietly. "He keeps to himself."

Charlotte's lips curved faintly. "Yes. I have noticed."

Silence fell again, broken only by the steady rhythm of the wheels against the rutted road. The maid's reserve began to chafe, for it was a reminder that even here in her own carriage, her husband's influence reached her.

"You are very careful with your answers," Charlotte said at last, turning back to Miriam. "Has His Grace instructed you not to speak freely?"

Miriam's hands folded more tightly in her lap. "No, Your Grace. Only... the Duke values discretion."

Charlotte regarded her for a long moment, then gave a small, rueful smile. "As do I, Miriam. But I also value honesty. Should I ask you something directly, I would prefer the truth, not the version you think will please him."

The maid's eyes lifted, uncertain but sincere. "Yes, Your Grace."

Charlotte nodded, satisfied enough, though the unease did not leave her. She leaned back against the seat, but the passing images were not enough to distract her. Behind her calm exterior, her thoughts churned.

She was married to a husband she barely knew. Together, they lived in a house full of rules and silences, among servants who spoke in careful half-truths. And the ghost of a man she once thought she loved was still haunting the streets she used to call home.

The carriage jolted as it turned onto the long road leading to Duskbourne Hall, as its grey silhouette rose against the clouds like something ancient and watchful. By the time the carriage rolled into Duskbourne's sweeping courtyard, the sky had faded to pewter.

Charlotte dismissed Miriam with a faint smile and a polite excuse about needing solitude. She needed to breathe without being observed, to think without the careful composure expected of a duchess.

The great hall was silent save for the slow tick of a clock and the distant murmur of servants in the kitchens. She hesitated at the base of the staircase. She could return to her chambers, or she could wander through the house that was now hers.

Her steps turned toward the east corridor almost of their own accord.

The air grew cooler there, scented faintly with old paper and smoke. She had intended to find the library, which the Duke had mentioned only briefly, but the directions had been lost in memory. The hallways stretched and branched like veins, throbbing endlessly around her.

You are not lost, she told herself quietly, though her steps slowed. *You are the mistress of this house. You cannot be lost.*

The sound of her own footsteps seemed almost impertinent in the hush. The deeper she went, the heavier the silence grew, as though the house were holding its breath.

It was then that she realized where her steps had carried her... the forbidden wing.

Her pulse quickened. Cassian's words came back to her with cold precision: *You are not to enter. Ever.* But something stronger than reason stirred in her chest. The silence here was different, not simply neglect but reverence. Grief, perhaps, preserved in air and dust.

For a long moment, she stood before the heavy double doors, her hand poised but not touching the latch. The wood was dark, the brass fittings dulled by age. Every instinct told her to turn away. And yet...

She pressed her palm against the handle, and it gave way with a soft, reluctant sigh.

The scent of old roses and faded linen met her at once, faint but unmistakable, as if the room had been sealed around a single memory. The light from the hall stretched thin across the floorboards, catching on motes of dust that drifted like ash.

She stepped inside.

The chamber was beautiful in its decay. A canopied bed stood beneath the window, with the drapes drawn halfway. A dressing table sat nearby, and its surface was scattered with small relics: a brush, a silver hand mirror, a perfume bottle long emptied. The fabric of a gown hung over a chair. It was pale ivory that had turned yellow with time.

On the far wall, she could see shelves of books that lined a small alcove. There were volumes of poetry and music, their spines faded from the sun that no longer reached them. All pointed to a woman's life, paused mid-breath.

And beside the hearth, half-hidden beneath a shroud of dust, stood a cradle. Charlotte's breath caught.

A child. His child.

She glanced around, half expecting that same child to jump out of one of the dark corners and waddle over to her, giggling. But dark silence soon swallowed that thought, and her lit candle focused on the curious object before her once again.

The cot was simple, carved of dark wood, and there was a fine blanket still folded within it. The sight pierced something deep in her, stirring a sadness she could not name.

Then, suddenly, she heard the unmistakable sound of boots striking stone. Charlotte froze, and she felt all the air leaving her lungs. The sound grew nearer, echoing down the corridor beyond the open door.

It was *him*. Of course it was.

Panic surged inside of her. It was too late for escape, too late even to hide the open door or her trespass. She stood motionless in the half-light of the shuttered room, surrounded by the ghosts of his past, feeling caught exactly where she had promised she would never be.

Chapter Ten

Cassian had been returning from his study, intending only to retire for the night, when a faint light caught his eye. His heart stilled momentarily.

The forbidden wing.

For a moment, he simply stared, as disbelief turned to a cold, swift fury that coursed through him like blood. Then he was moving, his stride in the rhythm of barely contained rage. The sconces along the hall seemed to shudder as he passed.

As soon as he reached the open door, he did not need to look inside to know. He could *feel* it, the disturbance in the air, the violation of something sacred.

He stepped through the threshold. Charlotte stood in the middle of the room, with her pale gown brushed by the dim light of the lamp she had dared to bring.

Cassian froze. "What do you think you are doing in here?" The words struck like lightning.

Charlotte stuttered. "I..."

"I gave you *one* command," he hissed, stepping closer, his anger finally breaking through the layers of discipline he wore like armour. "One! That you would *not* enter this wing!"

"I... I was lost, and I was looking for the library," she barely managed to reply. "Besides, this is my home now... You brought me into it, and you can't bar me from it."

"It is *not* your home!" The words burst from him before he could stop them. The outpour of rage was raw and violent, and there was no stopping it now. "Not this place and *certainly* not these rooms!"

Charlotte flinched, but she did not retreat. "Then what is it you guard so fiercely? What could be so terrible that I cannot even know it exists?"

He was taken aback by her question. It caused him to laugh, but it was a hollow, bitter sound that startled even him. "Why would you want to know?"

"I do," she told him. Her entire body seemed to be trembling before him, yet she refused to yield. "You shut every door between us, every question, every feeling, and call it duty. What are you hiding, Cassian? What could be worse than this endless silence?"

The name, *his name*, on her lips struck him like a blow. His fury snapped, giving way to something darker.

He turned from her, his hand dragging across the edge of the cradle as though to steady himself. "You want truth?" he demanded, feeling as though his heart was breaking all over again. "Then hear it. My wife died in this room. And my son... my only son, died before he ever drew breath."

Charlotte's eyes widened, and her lips parted in stunned silence.

Cassian's gaze burned into the portrait above the mantel. "This was *her* chamber. *Her* bed. *Her* books. It is *her* laughter that is woven into the walls of this house." His voice cracked, the edges splintering into grief. "And finally, this was, in a way, her mausoleum."

He turned on her then, his expression wild with fury and pain. "Are you happy now?"

Charlotte shook her head, utterly stricken by the truth. "I'm sorry, I didn't think—"

"Yes, you didn't *think*," he interrupted her furiously, still snarling. "You had no right to invade this place and to touch what is left of her."

He crossed the room in three strides and seized the lamp from her hand. Then he faced her one last time, with eyes that had never been colder or more distant.

"Do not ever come here again."

The door slammed behind him with a noise that threatened to destroy the entire house, yet it stood. He didn't care that he left her in complete darkness. For a moment, he stood on the other side, with his hands braced against the frame.

His eyes burned, though no tears came. He had not wept in years. He would not start now.

Cassian strode down the corridor until he reached the familiar door of his study. He entered, shutting it behind him with finality. He crossed to the sideboard, poured a glass with a trembling hand, and drank it down in one swallow. The liquid burned its way to his chest, but it did nothing to still the pounding in his skull.

Another pour. Another swallow.

He set the glass down too hard. It cracked at the base but held.

His gaze lifted to the fire. The flames licked at the grate, the same restless motion as the thoughts he could not suppress.

Her hands on Eleanor's things. Her eyes on that room.

He gripped the edge of his desk until his knuckles turned white. Charlotte had meant no harm. He knew that. But the very sight of her standing there amidst Eleanor's things had torn open something he had buried too deep to ever touch.

He saw it all again: the blood, the stillness, the physician's face, and finally, Eleanor's hand slipping from his. In a single moment of torment, he relived the night that had ruined every one to follow.

He pressed the heels of his palms against his eyes, forcing the memories back into the darkness where they belonged.

You cannot go back. You cannot fix it.

Then, a soft knock broke through his thoughts. He didn't say anything.

"Your Grace?" Her voice, quiet but trembling, drifted through the wood. "May I speak with you?"

He still said nothing. He could picture her on the other side of the door, small and uncertain, her hand perhaps still resting against the panel. The same woman who had looked at him with fire in her eyes moments ago now stood seeking forgiveness.

The thought tore at something inside him.

He drew a slow breath, straightened, and when he spoke, his voice was even, but cold enough to cut. "There is nothing to say, Duchess. Return to your chambers."

A pause. Then, she softly continued. "I only wished to say I'm sorry."

He shut his eyes. The words struck him like a knife. For one dangerous, human moment, he wanted to open the door and tell her that he knew she hadn't meant to wound him, that it was not her fault the past was made of glass and grief.

But he could not.

"Go," he said at last. "Please."

What followed was silence, then the faint sound of retreating footsteps fading down the corridor. Cassian's shoulders sagged. He sank into the nearest chair, his elbows braced against his knees. He stared into the fire until his vision blurred. The flames wavered, casting ghosts against the walls. Eleanor's silhouette intertwined with Charlotte's pale figure, two lives colliding in the ruin of one man's guilt.

He reached for the glass again, his hand unsteady this time. The brandy caught the firelight, dark and shining like spilled blood.

He drank.

The storm within him did not fade.

He feared that it never would.

***

"Are you ready?"

The words sounded strange, as they were the first three words he had said to her in the past two days. After so long, his voice sounded as if it belonged to someone else. Cassian waited in the doorway of Charlotte's chamber while she stood by her looking glass, making the final adjustments to her hair.

Slowly, Charlotte turned to face him. She had dressed for the afternoon in a gown of pale blue silk, her hair caught up in a coiffure less severe than her usual ones. She looked damningly beautiful.

"I am almost ready, Your Grace," she said carefully. "Although I didn't think you intended to accompany me."

Cassian met her gaze briefly, then looked past her, toward the polished wood of the doorframe. "It would be unseemly for you to attend your nephew's first birthday party without me.

One's private affairs should remain private, and this family celebration is hardly the place for speculation."

Her brow furrowed faintly. "Speculation?"

"The world loves a whisper of marital discontent, Duchess," he said curtly. "If we do not give them cause, they will invent one."

Charlotte blinked, clearly taken aback. "Of course," she murmured after a pause. "Thank you. I didn't expect—"

He cut her off before the sentence could form. "Do not thank me. I'm not doing this for you."

The words landed harsher than he intended, the edge sharper than he'd meant to draw. He saw the flicker of hurt in her eyes. It was there and gone in a heartbeat, and something in his chest twisted painfully.

Still, she inclined her head with quiet dignity. "Then I thank you for your consideration, Your Grace," she said softly.

Was that the faintest trace of irony in her tone he could trace? Not that it mattered.

Cassian looked away. "Be ready in ten minutes. We leave at the quarter-hour."

He turned sharply, heading down the corridor. He hated this necessity of cruelty, and even more, he hated the way it burned in him even as he wielded it. But distance was the only weapon he had left.

A few minutes later, Cassian found himself standing beside the carriage, with gloved hands clasped behind his back. The horses shifted restlessly as their breath steamed in the cold air of the afternoon. They could sense something, he was certain of it. When Charlotte appeared, wrapped in a dark cloak, he inclined his head.

"Shall we?"

She gave a small nod and let him help her into the carriage. Her fingers, cool against his, trembled just slightly. He released her hand as soon as decorum allowed and settled opposite her, signalling the driver without another word.

The road to Hawthorne was short, but neither of them spoke. The only sound was the steady rhythm of hooves and the low creak of the wheels. Charlotte was sitting with her profile turned to him, as if she had discovered something immensely eye-catching in the distance. Cassian told himself the silence was preferable, that it was safer this way.

When they arrived at Hawthorne House, the great house blazed with warmth and light. Cassian could not ignore the stark contrast between this home and his own. Servants came forward at once, and Nicholas himself met them at the steps.

"Duskbourne," Nicholas said with a nod. "Charlotte."

Cassian returned the greeting with equal civility. "Hawthorne." He offered his arm to his wife and led her up the steps with composed formality.

Inside, the air was bright with chatter and the faint scent of wine and sugared cakes. Lydia greeted them with genuine warmth. "You both made it! Charlotte, you look lovely. Your Grace, it's an honour as always."

Cassian inclined his head. "The honour is mine, Your Grace."

He felt Charlotte tense faintly beside him, perhaps feeling the weight of the guests' stares gathering near the doorway. So, he did what society demanded and what instinct compelled. He reached for her hand, threading his fingers through hers in a gesture of practiced ease. Her surprise was subtle but unmistakable.

The crowd's attention shifted almost imperceptibly. He had learned long ago how to control a room without raising his voice: one touch, one gesture, precisely timed.

When they were shown to their seats in the dining hall, he made certain to remain close beside her. He offered a word here, a polite smile there, playing his part to perfection. Yet every glance from her scraped at his composure like fine wire. It was easier to face Parliament than this.

He turned slightly toward her, his voice low enough for only her to hear. "You are trembling," he murmured. "Smile, Duchess. Everyone is watching."

Her lips curved so obediently and beautifully that the motion felt like a blade sliding between his ribs. As if it wasn't enough that this dinner was a glittering, suffocating affair. Laughter rang too loudly, candles burned too brightly, and Cassian felt as though every flicker of light in the room turned its gaze upon him. Still, he kept his composure, as always.

"Your Grace," Lydia said kindly, "I cannot tell you how delighted we are that you came. It has been far too long since we've seen you in society."

Cassian inclined his head with the faintest of smiles. "As I grow older, I prefer solitude, my lady."

Lydia laughed lightly, though her eyes darted to Charlotte. "Then perhaps Charlotte will change that."

Charlotte's fork stilled briefly against her plate before she replied. "I doubt even I could coax Duskbourne into the light."

Cassian turned his head slightly toward her. "Nor should you try, Duchess," he said evenly, the words polished but sharp beneath their courtesy.

A brief silence followed, one Lydia hastily filled with cheerful chatter about her son's first year. Cassian nodded in the right places, spoke when addressed, even smiled once or twice, but he could feel the weight of the room pressing down.

He could sense the subtle unease that always followed him, magnified now by the brittle tension between him and his new wife. No matter how perfectly he conducted himself, the strain beneath their façade felt visible, vibrating in the air like a drawn string. As he looked around the candlelit room, at the familiar faces and soft murmurs, he could not shake the certainty that every person there could see through him.

Chapter Eleven

To all appearances, it was a celebration of joy: the first birthday of the heir to the dukedom and also a day of familial bliss. To Charlotte, however, it felt like punishment.

She had practiced her smile before the mirror that morning, and even after all that practice, it did not reach her eyes. She stood near the nursery table where little Augustus was banging a silver spoon against his cup, shrieking with glee. A laughing Lydia swooped in to rescue both cup and child, looking radiant in her lavender gown. Charlotte joined her, but her laughter was strikingly different.

An hour had passed since luncheon, and the Duke was standing across the room. One needed to look no further to find a study in composure. His expression betrayed nothing, not even boredom, though she could feel the rigidity of his restraint even from where she was standing. They were husband and wife, bound by vows and proximity, yet they might as well have been strangers trapped in polite conversation.

When their eyes met by accident, Charlotte's chest tightened. He didn't even incline his head in acknowledgment. Then, he simply turned away to speak with her brother.

She swallowed against the ache that rose in her throat.

"Lady Duskbourne!" cried an elderly dowager, beaming as she approached. "My dear, what happiness it must be, newly wed and already an aunt to such a cherub!"

Charlotte curtsied, murmured the appropriate pleasantries, and kept on smiling until her jaw hurt. She could not recall a single thing the woman said. When the attention at last shifted elsewhere, she slipped toward the refreshment table. Her hand trembled slightly as she poured herself a glass of lemonade. The tartness bit at her tongue, and she accepted it as a small, bracing mercy.

"Charlotte?" Lydia's voice came softly from somewhere behind her.

Charlotte turned, extracting her practiced smile once again, though it wavered when she saw the concern in her sister-in-law's eyes.

"You needn't pretend with me, my dear," Lydia whispered gently.

"I beg your pardon?" Charlotte set down her glass carefully. "I have no idea what you are talking about."

Lydia's gaze softened, but she did not relent. "My dear, in all the years I have known you, I have come to see you as charitable, brave, and clever, but you have never been a convincing liar. I have been watching you with the Duke all evening. There is... *nothing* between you."

Charlotte felt her composure splinter, though she fought to keep her tone even. "You are mistaken. The Duke and I are—"

"—perfectly polite? Yes," Lydia finished for her gently. "Painfully so."

Humiliation scorched Charlotte's cheeks. She turned slightly, pretending to watch Augustus toddle across the rug toward his father's waiting arms.

Charlotte forced a smile, turning her attention back to Lydia. "Our marriage is as it was intended to be, one of mutual respect. We understand one another perfectly."

Lydia tilted her head, studying her with quiet pity. "Do you? Because from where I stand, you look like two people drowning, each too proud to reach for the other."

The words struck too close. Charlotte drew herself up, summoning dignity like armour. "Whatever exists between the Duke and myself is no one's concern but ours."

Lydia's expression softened further, and she appeared regretful now. "I did not mean to wound you. Only... you deserve happiness, Charlotte, not mere duty."

For a moment, Charlotte could not breathe. She pressed her fingertips to the rim of her glass, tracing it as though it might anchor her.

"I appreciate your concern," she said at last, endeavouring to calm down the tremble of her voice. "But some of us must learn to live content with duty."

Before Lydia could reply, Charlotte turned away. Her heart thudded painfully in her chest as she crossed the room, but her smile was once again carefully fixed in place. As if summoned by the weight of her thoughts, the Duke appeared at her side with that unerring sense of timing he had.

"Shall we offer our thanks to your brother before departing?" he murmured courteously, but he sounded as if he were discussing the weather.

Her pulse leapt. "We shall do no such thing."

One of Lydia's friends turned to glance at them, her smile all curiosity and gossip. Charlotte inhaled sharply, then slid her hand through her husband's arm.

"We shall walk," she announced slightly louder than she ought to have. "*Together.*"

If he was surprised, he did not show it. He inclined his head slightly, allowing her to lead. They crossed the room in a picture of marital harmony, then stepped out into the gardens.

Lanterns glowed along the gravel path, and the low murmur of conversation drifted from the terrace.

It was not privacy, but the illusion of it, and that was all society required.

They walked in silence, and she could feel the fabric of his coat brushing her bare wrist. Every nerve in her body seemed attuned to the smallest detail: the scent of him, which was an amalgamation of sandalwood and smoke, the warmth that radiated through the layers between them, and the quiet power coiled in his stillness.

When she could bear it no longer, she stopped abruptly.

"They are watching us," she said. "All of them. Every whisper, every look... I can feel it."

The Duke's gaze flicked toward the terrace where several figures lingered, feigning disinterest. "Let them watch," he replied with a shrug. "They will tire soon enough."

Her hand tightened on his arm. "No. They will not tire. They will speculate. They will say I am unhappy, or that you regret your choice. They will speak of pity and disappointment and all manner of things that are none of their concern, and I will not have it."

Something fierce glinted in his eyes. "And what would you have me do, Your Grace?"

She turned to face him fully, barely able to form the words that sent a blaze to her cheeks. "Kiss me."

His entire body stilled. "What?"

"Here. Now." Her voice was tremulous with both pride and challenge. "Kiss me, and silence them all."

A muscle palpitated in his jaw. "Charlotte..." He exhaled slowly. "You test my restraint."

"Then let it break," she whispered. "I can see you are still angry with me. Very well then, kiss me as if you are angry."

His gaze darkened, and for an instant, she thought he might turn away. Instead, he stepped closer, closing the narrow space between them.

"Be careful what you ask for," he murmured.

"I am not afraid."

"Perhaps you should be."

The words struck like a warning, but Charlotte did not retreat. Her pulse thundered in her throat. She could feel the heat of him and the tension thrumming between them like a drawn bowstring. He reached for her possessively, pulling her against him. She gasped, her palms pressing lightly to his chest.

His hand came to the back of her neck, with his fingers threading through her hair, and he kissed her.

It was no tender gesture. It was punishment, possession, fury, and yet beneath it, something ungovernable pulsed. The world tilted. Charlotte's breath caught as his mouth moved against hers, as though he would make her feel what he could not say.

Her hands on his chest felt the powerful rhythm of his heart. His lips softened, just barely, as if the fight drained from him for a single, impossible heartbeat. The moment undid her completely.

She tasted wine on his lips, and it filled her senses. The anger that had flared between them now twisted, becoming something else. It was confusion and longing and all the things she had forbidden herself to want.

When he tore himself back, the air between them was simmering, and yet, his hand was still at her waist, as if he could not quite bring himself to let her go.

"There," he said, his voice rougher than she had ever heard it. "Satisfied?"

Charlotte's lips parted. Her composure was in ruins. She wanted to slap him. Worse even, she wanted to kiss him again.

She smoothed her gown and forced a bout of air into her lungs. "That will do, Your Grace."

Composing herself with the icy precision that had become her shield, Charlotte turned toward the terrace. "We have been absent quite long enough," she murmured, not looking back.

He fell into step beside her.

As they entered the garden's edge, conversation faltered. Heads turned and fans fluttered, as they always did after a show. Laughter resumed a heartbeat too late, for it was the polite murmur of people who had just witnessed something they would spend the next week discussing over tea.

Charlotte's pulse thrummed in her ears. She could feel the eyes upon them still, but her expression was serene, as her arm looped neatly through her husband's. For now, she was the very picture of tranquil satisfaction.

They crossed the threshold together, their steps in tune. The crowd parted for them, murmuring admiration, curiosity, and, unavoidably, envy.

The rest of the evening passed as if behind glass: polished, suffocating, and distant. Charlotte continued to play her part beautifully. She was the devoted wife, the loving sister, and the affectionate aunt, and not a soul would have guessed the chaos that simmered beneath the surface.

When the hour grew late, the Duke murmured that it was time to depart. This time, Charlotte was grateful for the excuse. Together, they made their rounds, offering thanks, best wishes, and practiced smiles. Nicholas clasped the Duke's hand with brotherly warmth, while Lydia embraced Charlotte tightly.

Lydia leaned close enough for her breath to brush Charlotte's ear. "If you ever need me, you know where I am."

Charlotte drew back with a smile. "Everything is in perfect order."

Lydia's eyes lingered on her, but she said nothing more.

Moments later, Charlotte and the Duke stepped out into the night. The carriage awaited at the foot of the steps. While a footman opened the door, her husband offered his hand. His touch was brief and formal, but the contact sent a flicker of heat through her nonetheless, becoming a ghost of what had passed in the gardens.

Once the door closed and the carriage lurched forward, silence settled between them. Charlotte folded her hands in her lap. She could feel the tremor in them, faint but humiliatingly real.

At last, she drew a breath. "Your Grace... I owe you an apology."

He did not turn his head. "For what offense, precisely?"

"For disobeying you," she clarified, struggling to give voice to her thoughts. "For entering the west wing. I had no right."

She felt as though the words didn't have enough weight for the amount of regret she wanted to convey. She was truly sorry, and she wanted him to know it.

He drew in a slow breath, with his gaze still fixed on the dark window. "No, you did not."

"I did not mean to wound you," she continued, her throat tightening. "Only to understand—"

"Understand what cannot be undone?" His words cut through the air. "Curiosity may be natural, Charlotte, but it is a poor excuse to cross a boundary so clearly drawn."

A pause filled the air between them, long and taut.

"To understand you," she said at last, her voice soft. "And your pain."

He did not respond for some time, and she saw him swallow several times.

"I believe you are sorry," he said at last. "But understanding does not make your trespass itself vanish."

Charlotte looked down at her hands. "Then you cannot forgive me."

That was when he turned toward her, and the lamplight caught the faint silver at his temples. His expression was inscrutable, but his storm-lit eyes betrayed something almost human beneath the frost.

"I am trying to," he said quietly. "I want to forgive you. But wanting does make the past vanish. It is... hard."

It was not gentleness, not yet. It was effort. The strain of a man forcing civility against the pull of older wounds.

"Then I am grateful," she whispered.

He inclined his head, and some of the frost eased from his eyes. "Just know this, Charlotte. I do not wish to command you like a jailer, nor do I enjoy raising walls between us. But those secrets I guard... I keep them locked away because they are very difficult for me to remember."

What was this? An attempt at an apology? "I understand," she murmured.

"Do you?" he asked almost wearily. "I truly hope so. Because I would rather build a life with you than on opposite sides of locked doors."

The silence that followed was thick, but not empty. It pulsed with the memory of what had passed between them, that furious, breathless kiss neither could forget.

Cassian turned back to the window, while Charlotte faced forward. He was trying. She could see it now, in the restraint of his tone, and also in the measured distance he fought to keep.

But forgiveness, she knew, would not come easily.

Charlotte inhaled deeply, but it brought no relief. She would endure this, as she had endured everything. Yet deep within, under the hurt and pride, she could not banish the memory of his mouth on hers, and the suspicion that his anger was not the only fire still burning.

Chapter Twelve

Cassian had no idea how they had found themselves back in the garden, but this time, it was the middle of the night, and there was no one around.

Charlotte had her warm, trembling body pressed against his, and he already had a fistful of her luscious locks between his fingers. Her pert nipples pressed against him through the thin layer of her nightrail. Her lips were slightly swollen as she bestowed a coquettish glance upon him.

Had they been kissing? He had no idea.

Her hand slid down to his trousers, gripping his manhood.

"Charlotte, what—"

"Shhh," she whispered, lowering herself onto her knees.

She was fumbling with his belt, then the buttons. She couldn't possibly intend to...

He couldn't stop himself. None of this was proper, yet every instinct urged him to keep her close and never let go.

Then, her lips gently encircled the tip of his manhood. The touch was soft as her tongue swirled over him. The act obliterated his very ability to think. The world had dispersed into nothingness, leaving only the sight of her luscious lips closed around his manhood.

All his restraint dissolved. The animal inside had completely taken over, yet he knew he couldn't push her. He was ravenous for her, but he had to be patient. All he could do was watch her take him into her mouth deeper and deeper, playing with him. She moved slowly, teasing him, and the sight of him sliding in and out of her mouth almost made him finish right then and there.

When he opened his eyes and realized that he was in his bed, the remnants of his dream were so vivid that his pulse was unsteady.

For one disoriented moment, he could still feel her. Her scent was still on his fingers, something faintly floral. The whisper of her breath against his manhood still lingered, which now throbbed painfully, aching for release. In the dream, she had looked at him not with defiance, but with need. He had touched her as he'd sworn he never would touch another woman again: without caution, without distance, without reason.

He cursed loudly and sat up, dragging a hand through his hair. Cold air seeped through the crack in the shutters, mercifully sharp against his skin.

It was *intolerable*, this loss of control, this hunger that gnawed at him like a fever. He had built his life upon mastery of self. And yet one kiss, one reckless, infuriating kiss, had undone him.

He threw back the coverlet and rose, feeling the chill of the stone floor biting through to his very bones. He welcomed the discomfort. It was a reminder of who he was: a man governed by reason, not by weakness.

And *she* was his weakness.

She, with her stubborn pride and sharp tongue. She, who had disobeyed him, pried into the most sacred corner of his grief, and then stood before him unflinching.

He ought to despise her for it. So why did his body remember her as if she were burned into his very skin?

Cassian exhaled harshly and crossed to the washstand. He poured water into the basin, plunged his hands into it, and splashed his face until the cold drove the last of the dream away. His reflection stared back at him in the glass, until the same controlled, austere features society had come to expect of the Duke of Duskbourne had returned. No one would guess how easily he had been undone by his wife.

"Fool," he muttered under his breath.

He rang for his valet, who began to dress him. The familiar routine steadied him: linen shirt, waistcoat, coat, cravat tied with precision. By the time his valet fastened his cufflinks, his expression had settled once more into the cool indifference that served him as armour.

There was work to be done today... *real* work. The south fields required inspection after last night's rain, the stables needed review before the next shipment of horses to London, and Harrow awaited word on the tenant reforms before he could finalize the ledgers.

He would concern himself with *that*. He would focus on order, on progress, on the tangible world of duty. Certainly not on the woman who haunted his sleep.

By the time he reached the stables, the sun was a pale smear above the horizon. The stable hands straightened at his approach, offering bows and brisk greetings. Cassian returned them with curt nods, but he was already concentrating on the condition of the horses, the new feed supply, and the drainage near the paddock.

Business. Work. Order.

And yet, beneath it all, that same traitorous thought returned: how soft her mouth had been when she'd demanded he kiss her.

He pressed his lips together until the memory dulled.

Just as he had finished speaking with the head groom, he caught a flicker of movement at the edge of the courtyard. He recognized her immediately. She stood a few paces away, as morning light haloed her hair, turning it to gold. For a moment, Cassian could only look at her, struck by the incongruity of it: this delicate, graceful creature standing amid the scent of hay and damp earth.

"Your Grace," he greeted her first. "You are up early."

She hesitated before stepping closer. "I might say the same of you, Your Grace."

"I make a habit of beginning the day with my duties."

Her lips curved faintly. "Yes. So I have observed."

There was something in her voice, not mocking, but gentle and almost companionable. It unsettled him more than defiance would have.

"I wondered," she began carefully, "if I might accompany you on your walk through the grounds this morning. If it is not an intrusion, of course."

His first instinct was to refuse. That was the only way to keep their fragile peace untested by proximity. Also, the memory of his dream still lingered, uncomfortably vivid. But the hope in her eyes gave him pause.

"It is unorthodox," he said after a moment, "but not impossible."

"Then you consent?"

He hesitated, then nodded once. "If you wish it."

Her endearingly hesitant smile felt like sunlight breaking through fog. She fell into step beside him as he turned toward the path leading down toward the lower fields.

The morning air was cool and damp, and the grass was still heavy with dew. The faint cries of distant birds drifted from the moors. For a time, they simply walked in silence, nothing else. He kept his hands clasped behind his back, while she seemed to walk more lightly.

It was she who broke the silence first.

"The roses near the east wall are struggling," she pointed out. "I asked Mrs. Allen about them yesterday. She suspects the soil is too dry."

Cassian glanced at her briefly, surprised that she would notice something like that. "The gardener should attend to it. I will see that he does."

She nodded, looking faintly pleased. "Thank you. They were your late wife's, were they not?"

His step faltered. "Yes."

"I thought so," she murmured. "They are lovely. I should like to see them thrive again."

She spoke gently, without pity, and it disarmed him. He inclined his head slightly. "Then they shall."

Another pause followed. Birds wheeled above them, and the wind stirred her shawl.

"You know, I used to help my brother with the tenants' accounts when our father died," she said after a while, as though speaking more to the air than to him. "At first, I thought it dreadfully dull, all those columns and figures. But there was something strangely... satisfying in seeing order restored where there had been chaos."

Cassian's mouth curved faintly. "That actually sounds like me."

She glanced at him then, and for the first time in days, he did not look away. Her eyes were bluer and more bright than the sky that morning.

"Perhaps that is why we quarrel," she said as if pondering life's most important questions. "Two stubborn souls, both determined to be right."

He exhaled into a sound that was almost a laugh, though subdued. "That is not an impossible assessment."

They walked on. The tension that had hung between them like an invisible wire began to loosen. Her voice found a natural rhythm of small observations and small confidences.

"I used to think charity was something one did to soothe one's conscience," she admitted. "A kind of genteel performance. I suppose it was that way for me in the beginning. But when I began visiting the poorhouses regularly, when I started learning their names, their stories..." She paused, frowning slightly. "It ceased to feel like duty and became something else entirely. I cannot explain it, only that it feels more honest than most of what passes for virtue in society."

Cassian regarded her in profile, the faint crease between her brows when she grew thoughtful. "And yet," he said, "there are those who scorn you for it."

Her mouth twitched. He wished for a smile, but it was just weary acknowledgement. "Yes. There are whispers, of course. That I hide behind good works because I was too proud to wed when I had the chance. That my health failed. That I am half-mad, or penitent, or something equally romantic."

He arched an inquisitive brow. "Half-mad?"

Her eyes sparkled briefly. "Entirely uninteresting, I fear. I merely discovered that solitude can be... less lonely than false company."

It was the quiet recognition of a truth he knew too well. He found himself answering softly. "I understand that better than you might think."

Cassian suddenly turned from the valley, motioning toward a narrow path that curved behind the stables. "Come," he urged. "There is something I should like to show you."

She followed to a small clearing, bordered by ancient oaks. The ground was uneven, dotted with wildflowers and half-toppled stones. Near the centre stood the remnants of an old stone wall, its purpose now long forgotten.

"This," he said quietly, "was my kingdom once."

Charlotte turned to him, appearing puzzled. "Your *kingdom*?"

He gave a short, almost self-conscious smile. It was a rare, boyish expression that startled even him. "When I was a boy, my cousins and I would come here to play. We built a fortress of branches against that wall, fought imaginary battles, swore eternal oaths of loyalty."

Her eyes softened as she took in the sight. "How old were you?"

"Seven, perhaps eight." He paused, glancing around. "They left for the continent after my parents died, and I remained. I think I stopped coming here not long after."

She looked about the clearing with quiet reverence, as if seeing it through the eyes of a child: a secret world preserved in sunlight and memory.

"And you've not returned until now?"

"No." He shrugged. "There seemed little point."

That was when the first drop struck Cassian's sleeve. Another followed, then another. Within moments, the soft grey sky broke open, and rain came in a sudden, gleeful rush, not the usual polite drizzle of the English countryside.

Charlotte gasped as her hand flew to her bonnet. "Oh!"

Cassian could not help the low laugh that escaped him. "Come, quickly!"

They ran across the lawns, and laughter chased after them as quickly as the rain. Charlotte lifted her skirts, heedless of decorum and of the fact that her hair was coming loose in damp, golden curls. Cassian reached for her hand without thinking, and she took it.

By the time they reached the great doors of Duskbourne, both were soaked through. Charlotte's shawl clung to her shoulders, and his coat dripped steadily onto the marble floor. She was utterly breathless, her cheeks flushed, and her eyes bright with a light he hadn't seen before.

"I cannot remember the last time I was caught in the rain," she said between breaths, still smiling.

Cassian looked at her, feeling tension in his chest, as if a place was being created for her where he thought no one would dwell ever again.

"Nor I," he admitted, surprised to find himself grinning. "I cannot remember the last time I laughed at all."

Their smiles lingered, softening into silence. The sound of the rain filled the hall, drumming on the windows and pooling on the stone. They started toward the stairs together, still damp and still half-laughing.

Then, halfway up, Charlotte slipped. Her hand missed the banister, and her foot slid against the wet hem of her gown. In an instant, Cassian caught her, weaving his arm firmly around her waist and pulling her toward himself.

She gasped softly as her palms splayed against his chest. They froze, and between them, their breaths mingled. Her lips parted as though to speak, but no words came. Cassian could see the raindrops clinging to her lashes, then the quick rise and fall of her throat. His heart pounded in answer. He knew he should step back. He knew it as surely as he knew his own name. And yet...

Her fingers curled lightly in his soaked shirt. That small, unconscious movement undid him.

He bent his head, and their mouths met with no hesitation and no restraint. The kiss was deep, fierce, unthinking. It tasted of rain and warmth and every unspoken word between them.

Charlotte's breath caught against his lips. He could feel her hands trembling, sliding upward to his shoulders. For a moment, the world narrowed to the press of her body against his, the heat that flared even through wet fabric. He had completely given in to the desperate, beautiful wrongness of wanting what he had sworn never to want again.

She kissed him back as if it were the last kiss she would ever receive, and yet, he demanded more. Both of them were helpless in the face of their own desire, as his hands kept her close. Softly, she moaned against his mouth, and the sound sent a thunderous roaring through his insides. Her thigh pressed between his legs, feeling the length of his manhood throbbing with need.

His hand was on her breast, sliding underneath the fabric, feeling the scorching heat of her naked skin. There were so many layers to her chastity, and he felt he could tear them all off. His fingers found her pebbled nipple, and he could imagine how rosy-pink it would be. He imagined taking it into his mouth, playing with it, biting it gently, only to soothe the ache with his tongue again.

As if seeing that very image projected from his own mind, she sucked on his tongue, kissing him even harder. Nothing could dim the treacherous desire he felt for the woman he held in his hands.

Her thigh rubbed against his roaring manhood again, which was fighting to break free from the constraint of his trousers. His hand travelled down to her leg, grabbing a fistful of her gown, lifting it up. He yearned to touch the heat of her skin, even if it meant turning himself into flame.

His trembling fingers grazed her thigh, and she gasped softly. For one suspended moment, Cassian could hear nothing but the rush of his own heartbeat. Then, with a shuddering breath, he tore himself back.

And then, very suddenly, he released her as if burned, stepping away so abruptly she swayed where she stood. His hands curled into fists at his sides, which was a futile attempt to steady the chaos roaring through him. He had never seen her look more alive... and that was precisely the danger.

He clenched his jaw, forcing the words through gritted teeth. "You should change," he instructed, swallowing heavily. "You'll catch your death standing here."

Charlotte blinked, and confusion flickered in her eyes before it hardened into composure. "Of course," she murmured. "As you wish, Your Grace."

He meant to say something more, something that would soften the chill between them, but the words refused to come.

It was better this way. *Better distance than temptation.*

As she turned, he caught the faintest trace of disappointment in her expression. Then she gathered her soaked skirts and ascended the stairs without another word.

She was his wife, yet he had no right to her, not while the ghosts of his past still stood between them. He would destroy her if he gave in, the way he destroyed everything he loved.

Chapter Thirteen

"I cannot think what has possessed you, my dear," Lydia declared, pinning a swatch of silk to the wooden frame with the air of one pronouncing judgment upon the world. "You have pricked your finger three times and tied the same ribbon into a knot that no living soul could undo. Surely something dreadful must be occupying your mind."

Charlotte was seated opposite with a basket of thread in her lap, and she was utterly unsuccessful at attempting composure. "Nonsense. I am merely unpractised."

"You have been *unpractised* these past two hours," Lydia retorted. "Do not insult my intelligence."

The little workroom smelled faintly of dye and starch. Afternoon light filtered through the tall windows of Lydia's textile shop, or her *enterprise,* as Nicholas called it with affectionate dismay. Bolts of muslin and satin were neatly arranged along the wall, and two seamstresses worked industriously nearby, pretending not to hear.

Charlotte sighed and laid down her needle. "I am distracted, that is all."

"Indeed? And what, pray, is the name of your distraction? I suspect it answers to 'the Duke of Duskbourne.'"

"Lydia!" Charlotte hissed, glancing toward the maids. "Must you always be so direct?"

"It saves time." Lydia plucked a thread from her gown and smiled with too much innocence. "Now, tell me why you are sitting there like a heroine in the third act of a tragedy. Did he offend you? Did he fail to notice your new bonnet?"

Charlotte's lips curved despite herself. "No. He has noticed me more than enough, I fear."

"Ah." Lydia leaned forward, and as she did so, her eyes lit up with curiosity. "Now we approach the heart of it."

Charlotte hesitated, her fingers twisting in the folds of her skirt. "Our marriage..." She faltered. "It is not what people imagine it to be."

"Meaning?"

"It is a performance," Charlotte said softly. "For the world. For society. We are cordial, even kind, but it is not—"

"Romantic?" Lydia supplied.

"Real," Charlotte finished, ignoring her. "At least, it was not meant to be."

Lydia regarded her for a moment, head tilted. "And yet you look as though it has lately become more complicated."

Charlotte turned away, feeling her cheeks warming. "Do you recall the birthday celebration?"

"My son's grand fête? I should hope so, I planned it," Lydia said, amusedly. "Though, if you refer to *that kiss*, I daresay the entire county remembers it, too."

Charlotte groaned. "Do not remind me."

Lydia's grin widened. "My dear, it was *most* convincing. Nicholas declared afterward that it was the first time he had seen you two appear truly in love. I did not have the heart to tell him you looked ready to faint."

Charlotte covered her face with her hands. "Oh, Lydia, that is precisely the trouble."

Lydia laughed. "That you fainted?"

"That it felt real."

That silenced her sister-in-law for a moment. "Real?"

Charlotte nodded, lowering her hands. "I do not know what came over me. It was supposed to mean nothing, just means to silence gossip, nothing more. And yet..." She trailed off, staring down at the half-finished embroidery in her lap. "I cannot stop thinking about it."

Lydia's eyes softened. "Oh, Charlotte."

"I keep telling myself it was anger, or obligation, or some strange impulse brought on by the moment," Charlotte continued. "But when he kissed me, it did not feel false. And now—" She broke off, pressing her lips together.

"And now you wish it had," Lydia finished gently.

Charlotte gave a helpless little laugh. "Yes. That would be far simpler."

Silence stretched for a moment, filled only by the rustle of fabric and the ticking of the mantel clock.

Then, very quietly, Charlotte added, "You know, sometimes I wonder what it would be like... to share more than appearances with him. Even though I never meant to."

Lydia raised a brow. "Do you mean...?"

Charlotte's flush deepened. "Do *not* make me say it."

"Oh, I quite insist," Lydia teased. "It is not every day my virtuous sister-in-law confides such dangerous curiosities."

Charlotte clasped her hands together, feeling mortified. "I simply wonder what it would be like to be his wife in truth. I do not mean to change our agreement. I only..." She paused, her voice a whisper now. "I only wonder."

Lydia tried, and failed, to suppress a mischievous smile. "My dear, you sound precisely as I did before Nicholas and I—"

"Lydia!" Charlotte covered her ears, horrified. "You cannot possibly mean to speak of my brother in such a context!"

Lydia laughed outright. "You asked for honesty!"

"I asked for sympathy, not indecency!"

"Very well," Lydia said, still laughing, "but allow me to say this much: curiosity is not a sin, Charlotte. Denial, however, can be a very dull sort of virtue."

Charlotte lowered her hands, with her cheeks still aflame. "You are incorrigible."

"And you," Lydia said affectionately, "appear to be smitten by your husband."

Charlotte met her gaze, startled. "I am not—"

"No?" Lydia's tone softened, and the teasing was slowly fading into warmth. "Then why do you look so very much like a woman who *is*?"

At last, when the amusement had dwindled into soft sighs, Lydia leaned back in her chair.

"My dear," she said gently, "you must decide what you want."

Charlotte blinked. "What I want?"

"Yes." Lydia folded her hands neatly in her lap as she spoke. "You speak of your husband as if he were a distant star: too far to reach and too bright to look upon. But he is a man,

Charlotte. And men, even the most solemn of them, are rarely won by silence."

Charlotte frowned, her fingers tracing the edge of her embroidery hoop. "You make it sound so simple."

"It is not simple," Lydia allowed, "but it is clear. If you want something, show him."

Charlotte looked up sharply. "*Show* him?"

Lydia's smile turned knowing. "Do not look so scandalized. I do not mean you should throw yourself at him in the corridor, though if you did, I confess I should admire your courage."

"Lydia!"

"Well, I should." Lydia laughed softly, but her gaze was kind. "I mean only that men often require direction where feelings are concerned. If your husband believes you wish only for civility, he will give you civility. If he thinks you desire friendship, he will offer precisely that. But if you wish for... *more*..." She lifted her brows in quiet challenge.

Charlotte felt her pulse quicken. "You make it sound like a negotiation."

"Marriage always is," Lydia said. "Even the happiest ones. You must decide what you are willing to risk."

Charlotte looked down at her hands, the fine tremor of her fingers betraying her composure. "And if I risk it and fail?"

"Then you will at least know you were brave." Lydia's voice softened. "Do not spend your life wondering what might have been if you had reached out once more instead of turning away."

For a long moment, Charlotte said nothing. She simply stared down at the tangled thread in her lap and thought of

Cassian's eyes, the warmth of his hand, and the way his laughter had sounded in the rain.

When she looked up again, her cheeks were flushed, but her eyes were steady. "Perhaps you are right."

***

By the time Charlotte's carriage rolled through the great iron gates of Duskbourne, Lydia's words had settled in her mind like a spark refusing to die.

If you want something, show him.

The phrase repeated itself as she entered the quiet halls and as her maid helped her undress from her day gown. She was tired of walking on eggshells around a man who made her heart ache merely by existing across a room.

She was his wife, after all. And though their union had been founded on convenience and duty, surely there was no harm in claiming a sliver of warmth within it.

By the time the clock in the corridor chimed ten, she had made her decision.

Charlotte stood before the looking glass, studying the reflection that stared back: her hair was loosely gathered, and there were a few curls escaping at her neck. Her wrapper of pale ivory silk was unfastened just enough to suggest, not reveal. The sight made her heart race; partly out of fear, partly out of something far more dangerous.

Carrying a tray with two cups of tea, she walked down the corridor toward Cassian's study. The house was quiet, save for the steady whisper of rain against the windows. Light glowed beneath his door. It assured her it would be all right to knock, which she did.

His voice came from inside. "Come in."

He looked up as she entered, and surprise flickered briefly across his features. He sat at his desk, with papers lying before him in neat order, though his cravat hung loosely, as though he'd grown tired of formality.

"Forgive the intrusion," she said lightly, setting down the tray. "You have been closeted here all evening, and I thought you might wish for tea."

He regarded her a moment before nodding. "Thank you."

Charlotte poured for them both, careful not to spill. The silence stretched thin.

"You work too late," she said at last, striving for ease. "Even your tenants would scold you for such dedication."

A faint curve touched his mouth. "I doubt they would dare."

"Perhaps they should. A little rebellion is healthy."

He glanced up at that. "Do you speak from experience?"

"Possibly." She smiled and dared to step closer, although her entire body was trembling from being so near to him. "Do you ever tire of being obeyed so completely, Cassian?"

He stilled at her use of his name, for it was a small intimacy that seemed to hang in the air between them.

"Obedience," he said slowly, "has its comforts."

Charlotte tilted her head. "And its loneliness."

For a moment, neither moved. The firelight painted soft shadows across his features. His gaze flicked to the loose curl brushing her collarbone.

Encouraged, she took another step forward. "It is a dreary thing, I think, to be forever proper."

"Dreary," he echoed, though his voice had grown quieter. "Perhaps."

"Would you prefer a little rebellion, then?" she asked, her tone light but trembling faintly at the edges.

That was when something in his expression shifted. It was not exactly anger, but alarm. He rose from his chair with a movement that was controlled yet sharp at the same time.

"Perhaps you should retire. It is late."

Her heart fluttered painfully. "I am not tired."

"Nonetheless." He moved past her, toward the hearth, as though distance might steady him. "It would be best."

She turned, confused, hurt, prickling at her throat, and making it difficult to speak. "Have I offended you?"

He looked at her then, and she saw the truth he tried to hide. The storm was barely contained in his eyes.

"No," he said at last. "Only... this is not—" He broke off, closing his eyes briefly as if to master himself. When he spoke again, his tone was impersonal. "You are my wife, Charlotte. You deserve respect. And I would not... misuse that."

The words struck like cold water. She had come prepared for rejection, but it hurt more than she had anticipated.

"I see," she said quietly. "Then I shall not trouble you further."

He turned toward her, as if to speak, but she was already moving to the door. Her fingers trembled slightly on the handle, though her voice remained steady. "Good night, *Your Grace.*"

The title landed between them like a wall. She left without looking back.

Once safely back in her chamber, she closed the door and pressed a hand to her chest, willing her breath to steady. The flush on her cheeks was not only humiliation. It was also heat that refused to fade despite his rejection.

For all his coldness, she had seen it: the flicker of want he had fought to hide.

It was small comfort, and yet, it was enough to keep her awake long after the lamps were extinguished, her mind caught between wounded pride and the dangerous thrill of knowing she might not be alone in her longing.

Chapter Fourteen

Sleep did not come easily that night.

Cassian lay awake long after the house had gone still and the fire in his grate had faded to embers. Every time he closed his eyes, he saw her. The scent of tea and rain still clung to his thoughts.

He had wanted her. God help him, he had wanted her so fiercely that for a single, dangerous instant, all the walls he'd built since Eleanor's death had nearly collapsed. When she had stepped closer, he'd felt that wild, reckless pull he was trying so hard to resist.

And still, he had turned away.

It had been the only choice left to him. To give in would have been to lose what little control he still possessed. And yet, as he lay there, staring into the dark, he could not escape the quiet certainty that he had wounded her.

Charlotte.

She was unlike anyone he had met before. Hers was a soul that was too proud to beg, too clever to flatter, and too alive to remain confined within the cold boundaries he had drawn for her. He had thought this marriage of convenience would be a reprieve: duty without danger, companionship without risk. Instead, it had become a battlefield he was losing by degrees.

By dawn, he gave up all pretence of rest.

He rose, got dressed, and went riding hard across the fields until the wind cut through the fog in his head. But even there, amid the heather and the mist, he found no peace.

As the day passed, he threw himself into the work of the estate with ferocious purpose. He rode the boundaries, met with tenants, reviewed accounts until his eyes ached... *anything* to keep from thinking of her.

However, it was at his club nearly a week later that the first whisper reached him.

"Tragic thing, Duskbourne's marriage," one gentleman murmured as Cassian passed.

"... to lose them both like that..." another whispered.

"Aye, no wonder he has gone mad."

"They say he was never quite the same."

"Then it is no wonder he cannot consummate the match! He has been left quite impo—"

The sentence broke off the moment he entered the room. The laughter that had filled the air seconds before stilled into polite silence. Cassian's gaze swept over them. It was a quiet, withering glance that sent several men scurrying to their cards.

He said nothing. He did not need to. But the words had already landed.

By the time he returned to Duskbourne, the rumour had sprouted like weeds. A servant's sidelong glance here, a faltering curtsy there. They were small things, but unmistakable. The walls of his own house seemed to hum with speculation.

He confronted the butler first.

"Mr. Tarrow," he inquired of the man, "I should like to know who has been speaking of matters that are not their concern."

The butler blanched. "Your Grace, I assure you—"

"Assure me of nothing," Cassian cut in. "You know very well that I do not care for whispers within my household. If I hear another syllable of this nonsense, I will see the entire staff dismissed and replaced by those with more discretion."

Tarrow bowed deeply, trembling. "Yes, Your Grace. It shall be seen to at once."

Cassian turned away, fury coiled in his chest. However, it was not the clean, sharp kind he was used to, but something slower, more corrosive. It was not merely the gossip that enraged him. It was what it revealed: how deeply he cared that anyone might think Charlotte unloved and undesired.

He had thought himself above such things.

And yet, the idea that her name might be pitied, or that anyone might imagine her neglected, or, God forbid, unwanted, made his blood burn.

He had to do something about it, and the first chance he got was when he found her the next morning in the breakfast room. She sat alone at the table, with a book open before her and an untouched tea cooling at her elbow. When she looked up at his entrance, he saw the faintest flicker of unease cross her face, almost as if she didn't want him there but had to endure his presence.

"Good morning, Your Grace," she greeted him politely, but without any emotion.

He hesitated. The formal address stung more than it should have.

"Charlotte, it's good I found you here," he said at last.

She closed the book carefully. "You wished to speak with me?"

"I did." He crossed the room and stopped before her, his hands clasped behind his back. It was easier to begin with control and to let precision do what gentleness could not. "It has come to my attention that certain rumours are circulating... about *us*."

Her brows drew together. "Rumours?"

"Yes." His mouth tightened, having glanced around the chamber one more time, to assure himself they were alone. "That our marriage has not been... consummated."

For a moment, she said nothing. Then, she softly concluded, "I see."

He caught the quick rise of colour in her cheeks and the flash of anger that followed.

"And you imagine this began within your club?" she inquired calmly.

"I imagine it began *here*," he said grimly. "Servants talk. Secrets spread. And once they reach the drawing rooms of London, they acquire an ugliness all their own."

Charlotte looked away. "So, we are to be a scandal again," she said quietly. "How efficient of us."

"Charlotte—"

"No, I understand." She looked up, meeting his gaze squarely now. "You mean to say we must convince them otherwise."

Her tone carried no mockery, only a weary sort of irony. Cassian drew a breath, forcing himself to speak plainly. "Yes. The whispers must end. They will damage you far more than me."

Her chin lifted slightly. "You are thinking of my reputation."

"Yes, I am thinking of yours," he said. "And of the household. We cannot have gossip poisoning the air we live in."

There was a pause. Then, with a steadiness that surprised him, she asked, "What do you propose?"

Cassian hesitated. The question was simple enough, yet his mind supplied only images: her hand slipping from his arm that night in the rain, her voice trembling in his study, and the disappointment in her eyes.

He forced his thoughts into order. "We must appear—" he stopped, then chose the words with care, "content and familiar. As though there was no distance between us."

Charlotte regarded him without revealing a single thing about her own emotions. "A convincing picture of intimacy, you mean."

"Yes."

"In public and even here, in our own home."

He inclined his head. "*Especially* here. Servants observe more than they should. Let them see us dine together, walk together, sit together in the evenings. Small gestures will suffice."

"And if small gestures do not?"

His gaze met hers. The question hung between them, charged with meaning.

"Then we shall do what is necessary," he said quietly.

"Very well," she concluded after a moment. "If we are to play the part, we must do it convincingly."

Cassian almost smiled, but he managed to resist the urge. "You sound almost eager."

"I am practical," she replied with a composed shrug. "If society insists upon peering through the windows of our marriage, then let them see what they expect."

He admired her for the steadiness with which she said it. He could see the calm poise that masked what must surely cost her to discuss so openly.

"Then we are agreed," he said.

"Yes," she murmured. "Agreed."

***

At first, it felt like theatre.

Cassian had endured such performances before, but this was the hardest of them all. He was unable to escape the polished civility of Parliament or the intricate falsehoods of London society, but this was something different. This was intimate deception, staged not before strangers, but beneath the roof that was meant to be his sanctuary.

Their new arrangement began that evening.

When he entered the dining room, Charlotte was already seated. Two places were laid side by side, rather than across from one another, as had been their unspoken custom since their wedding. The servants had done as instructed. Every detail of the setting suggested domestic harmony.

Cassian took his seat beside her. The distance between them was narrow enough that he could sense the faint warmth of her arm through the fine fabric of her sleeve.

"Good evening," she said, with as much composure as she could manage, but he could see her fingers twisted once in her napkin before she stilled them.

"Good evening," he replied.

They spoke, at first, of harmless things, while the diner was being served.

"The west fields seem improved since the new rotation," Charlotte remarked, her voice even, her eyes fixed on her plate.

"Indeed," Cassian replied. "The tenants at Greythorne reported a larger yield this quarter. I mean to visit them next week."

"Without Mr. Harrow?"

He glanced at her. "Gideon has business in London. I can manage a field inspection without supervision."

Her lips curved faintly. "You might even enjoy it."

He almost smiled. "Doubtful."

A brief silence fell while the footman poured the claret. Charlotte reached for her glass at the same instant he did. Their fingers brushed in what was just a whisper of contact, but it was enough to still the air between them.

"Forgive me," she murmured.

"There's nothing to forgive," he said quickly. His tone was composed, but his pulse betrayed him.

It was absurd, he told himself. Such a simple gesture, meaningless even. And yet, as the meal continued, every small proximity seemed suddenly magnified. When the servants were near, she smiled more easily, and her tone sounded warmer. Again, as she reached for the salt, her sleeve brushed his wrist, light as breath. He could not have said whether she did it by accident or design.

Later, as they stood together in the drawing room for the servants' benefit, Charlotte lifted a book from the table and made some idle remark about the author. He leaned closer to answer and caught the faint tremor of her breath. She turned slightly toward him, her eyes meeting his. The distance between them vanished for a heartbeat.

Then, it was time for the big finale.

By the time the clock struck midnight, she was there, in *his* bed chamber, a pale figure in candlelight. Her maid had drawn back the curtains and banked the fire, leaving the room cast in a dim, amber glow. Cassian had dismissed his valet early and was sitting by the hearth with a book open but unread in his lap.

"Will this arrangement suit you, Your Grace?" she asked lightly, though he detected the faint tremor beneath her composure.

"It will suffice," he said. His tone was deliberately neutral, though the sound of his voice grated even on himself.

When she slipped beneath the coverlet, she looked impossibly good in his bed. He extinguished the lamp and lay beside her, but the space between them felt narrow and insufficient. The bed, once so cavernous, now felt intolerably small.

Her warmth radiated through the few inches that separated them, and with it came the faintest trace of lavender and clean linen, the scent that seemed, of late, to haunt him everywhere. Cassian lay rigid, staring into the darkness. Charlotte exhaled softly beside him. Then, in the restless turning of half-sleep, she shifted. Her back brushed his arm, and it was enough to send a shock through him. Every nerve in his body flared to life. He gritted his teeth, forcing stillness. His mind supplied a dozen reasons to move, but his body betrayed him.

He stayed.

And so he lay there, not sleeping, not daring to move, with the scent of her hair in the dark and the sound of her breathing threading through every thought until dawn.

When the light finally broke through the curtains, he felt as though he had not closed his eyes all night.

A soft knock sounded at the door, followed by the familiar voice of his valet. "Your Grace?"

Before either of them could reply, the door opened. The valet froze, his eyes widening.

Charlotte stirred beside him, like a well-rested cat. "Good morning," she said. "You may leave the tray on the table."

Cassian pushed himself up on one elbow, feigning indifference though his heart pounded absurdly fast. He caught the flash of astonishment and triumph in the valet's expression before he bowed and retreated.

For a moment, neither of them spoke. Then Charlotte swung her legs out of bed, reaching for her robe.

"Well," she said lightly, "I daresay that will do for appearances."

Cassian forced a faint smile. "It would seem so."

But as he watched her knot the sash of her robe, her face turned slightly away, he felt an odd, hollow ache. She did not look at him again.

All that morning, through breakfast and the day's appointments, she was polite but distant. It was that cool civility which stung far more than anger.

He told himself it was nothing. That her composure was a shield, as his was. Yet some part of him knew better.

Perhaps she still resented him for turning her away that night in his study. Or perhaps she felt trapped in this playacting, forced into intimacy without affection.

Whatever the reason, he could feel her slipping from him, and the irony struck deep.

He had drawn every boundary, built every wall.

And now, when she stood just within reach, he was the one left wanting.

Chapter Fifteen

The letter arrived on a Wednesday morning, borne upon the usual tray of correspondence and estate accounts. Charlotte might not have noticed it at all if not for the handwriting. It was that looping, self-assured scrawl that had once made her heart leap whenever it appeared upon an envelope, and she recognized it instantly.

Mr. Edmund Larke.

For a moment, she only stared at the name, with her teacup suspended midway to her lips. The sound of the clock ticking in the corner filled the silence. Even the maid, arranging flowers by the window, seemed suddenly too loud.

Charlotte set the cup down with care. Her first impulse was to tear the letter in half, unread. But that old, dangerous weakness aptly named curiosity stilled her hand.

The seal was a deep green, pressed clumsily. It was not the colour he used before. He must have run out of his usual wax. It struck her as fitting somehow: theatrical, but careless.

Breaking it, she unfolded the paper.

My dearest Charlotte,

I cannot pretend to forget you. Not a day has passed since our cruel parting that your image has not haunted my mind. You were, and still are, the light of my life, the only woman who ever truly understood me. I have heard of your marriage to the Duke of Duskbourne (though I cannot bring myself to write his name without bitterness). Surely such a cold alliance cannot content a heart like yours. Say the word, and I will come for you. We can still be free, you and I.

Ever yours, in life and in longing,

Edmund Larke

Charlotte's first reaction was not anger, nor sorrow, but rather astonishment at the sheer audacity. He had discovered her husband's name and her address. He had written to *Duskbourne Hall*, as if she and he were still partners in some foolish romance rather than strangers joined only by a shared humiliation.

She folded the letter neatly, pressing her thumb along the crease. Once, such words would have undone her. Once, she would have read them through tears, believing every extravagant phrase, every promise of devotion. But now, they seemed pitifully hollow.

The handwriting that once thrilled her looked overwrought. The endearments that had once felt like poetry now struck her as cheap imitation. Even the memory of his voice stirred only faint disgust.

She had thought herself ruined by him, condemned to live forever in the shadow of her own foolishness. Yet as she sat there, sunlight slanting across the page, Charlotte realized she felt nothing. Not even the faintest flicker of that old ache. Whatever flame had once burned for Edmund Larke had long ago gone out.

Charlotte set the letter aside on the table, laying it neatly upon the tray with the morning's correspondence. She told herself she would dispose of it later, perhaps after tea, when the servants were busy elsewhere and no one might see. For now, she wished only to forget it existed.

She had just turned toward the window when the door opened.

Cassian entered, greeting her politely.

"Good morning," she returned, schooling her tone to calm.

He moved to the sideboard, glancing over the tray of letters with his usual habitual precision. "Has the post arrived?"

"Yes, but nothing of importance."

He reached for the uppermost envelope before she could stop him.

The sight of Cassian's hand on that green seal sent her heart lurching.

"Cassian—"

But it was too late. His gaze had already fallen on the name scrawled across the front. His expression changed, and there was the faintest flicker of disbelief that hardened, almost instantly, into something far sharper.

He opened it quickly and read it.

Charlotte felt her stomach twist. "That letter was not meant—"

"For me?" he finished coldly, still reading. "No, I should think not."

When he looked up, his eyes were dark with a kind of controlled fury.

"Edmund Larke," he said, each syllable like a stone. "Some sort of a wishful poet?"

"He is nothing to me," Charlotte said quickly. "He wrote without my invitation. I only meant to—"

"Burn it?" Cassian's mouth curved in a humourless smile. "A noble thought, though you seem to have delayed in carrying it out."

Her cheeks flushed. "I had every intention of doing so."

He set the letter down sharply. "You should not have read a word of it, once you have seen where it was headed."

"I did," she said, more steadily now. "And I found it absurd."

He gave a short, disbelieving laugh. "Absurd? The man declares undying devotion to my wife, even promises to whisk you away like some sentimental highwayman, and you call it *absurd*?"

"Because it is!" she retorted, feeling her temper rising. "We used to exchange silly letters a while back, and I thought... well, I thought him something he was not. I no longer care for him, and he is a fool for imagining I ever could again."

Cassian stared at her. She could see anger in his eyes. "You once did," he reminded her.

She drew herself up. "*Once*. I was naïve. But I have learned."

He seemed to search her face for the truth, then looked down again at the letter. As he did, a small, folded slip of paper slid from within.

He caught it before it fell to the floor and unfolded it with an impatient hand.

"Ah," he said flatly. "He also included a poem. How fitting."

Before she could stop him, he began to read aloud, and his tone was edged with mockery.

"The rose doth blush, ashamed beside thy cheek,

The moon grows faint, its silver seeming weak,

The stars themselves conspire to dim their flame,

For none may shine beside thy sainted name.

Had I but wings, I'd fly from shame and scorn,

To lay my life before thee, love forlorn,

To steal thee, my heart's last, reckless plea,

And bind our fates through love's eternity."

He broke off with a sound that was halfway between a laugh and a scoff. "Good God. I should think even his rhymes are false."

Charlotte, despite herself, felt the corner of her mouth twitch. "It is dreadful," she admitted, "though the rhythm is pleasant."

"The rhythm?" Cassian repeated in disbelief. "My dear, the man cannot manage a proper meter if his livelihood depended upon it, which, in fact, it does."

"Still," she said lightly, "it is not wholly without charm."

"Charm?" He looked at her as though she had insulted the entire canon of English verse. "There are *actual* good poems in existence, Charlotte. This is drivel."

Cassian held the sheet at arm's length as though it offended him.

"Roses, moons, and stars," he snarled at the poem. "A parade of sentiment without a single thought behind it. How does he imagine himself a poet?"

Charlotte's lips twitched despite the tension between them. "You are very severe, Your Grace."

"I am honest," he replied. "If the man had read anything finer than a valentine in his life, he would not abuse the language so."

"Perhaps he meant to please the heart, not the intellect."

Cassian turned toward her, with one brow raised. "A poem that does neither is fit only for the fire."

She laughed softly, shaking her head. "You are impossible. You despise every feeling that cannot be measured."

"On the contrary," he said quietly, "I despise only the counterfeit of feeling."

Something in his tone made her breath catch. He regarded her a moment longer, then crossed to the bookcase.

"Here," he said, taking down a worn volume bound in dark green leather. "If you will suffer a true poem, you may hear what beauty sounds like when it does not lie."

He opened the book with the ease of habit, finding the page at once. His voice, when he began, was low but resonant, the words carrying an old gravity.

"Love is not love which alters when it alteration finds,

Nor bends with the remover to remove,

O no! It is an ever-fixed mark,

That looks on tempests and is never shaken."

Charlotte stilled, and the air itself seemed to thrum. He went on, the cadence steady, his voice deepening as though the poem itself passed through him.

"Love's not Time's fool, though rosy lips and cheeks

Within his bending sickle's compass come,

Love alters not with his brief hours and weeks,

But bears it out even to the edge of doom."

When he finished, she couldn't find the words. Cassian closed the book slowly.

"*That*," he said, his eyes still fixed on her, "is what words can do."

Charlotte could hardly draw breath. She knew the sonnet, of course. But hearing it read by him made it even more beautiful. There was something in the way he looked at her, as though the poem were no longer Shakespeare's, but his own confession spoken through borrowed lines.

"Yes," she whispered. "It is… beautiful."

He stepped closer, his gaze never leaving hers. "It endures because it is true."

He was close enough that she could feel the warmth of him, pointing to the open page still in his hand.

"See there," he murmured, "how the line carries the weight, not of sweetness, but of constancy. It holds."

She could barely follow his meaning. His hand brushed hers as he showed her the lines, and she felt the world tilt slightly. The pulse in her wrist quickened under his fingertips. When she lifted her eyes, he was already looking at her not as a duke, nor a husband bound by duty, but as a man fighting something he could no longer reason away. The air between them was so charged it seemed the poem itself breathed.

He was standing so close to her that she could feel his hot breath on her skin. But no matter how desperately she wanted him to kiss her, she knew that he wouldn't.

Instead, he brushed his nose against hers, driving her mad. "Lie down," he whispered.

Her eyes widened in surprise. "What?"

His hand gently pushed her back toward the chaise lounge.

"Lie down." He repeated his command, and a million little goosebumps ran down her back.

She could barely control her breathing as her entire body trembled. Without even realizing she had done it, her body rested on the softness of the chaise lounge. Cassian then knelt in front of her.

"What do you mean to—"

"Shhh." That was all he told her, not taking his eyes off of her.

Charlotte had no idea what to think. In fact, she *couldn't* think. Not when she felt Cassian's fingers lift the hem of her gown, revealing her bare legs. Strangely, she felt no shame. All she could feel was a sense of rightness about the moment, whatever it was to bring next.

Suddenly, heat unfurled from somewhere deep inside of her, and all she could do was watch him with his mischievous grin as he lowered a reverent kiss to her inner thigh. It was as if he had scorched her with fire, yet she didn't move. She wanted more... so much more.

His hands gently coaxed her to open more for him, and she did. She bit her lip, wondering if he was truly going to do what she thought he would.

"Cassian," she murmured his name through a moan. "You can't possibly mean to—"

"Shhh," he urged again, and his mouth pressed once more into her naked skin.

He continued trailing a line of kisses up her thigh until he found what he was looking for.

"Oh..." she moaned, louder this time, feeling as his tongue stroked over her most intimate flesh.

She looked down at his ruffle of dark hair and gripped it tightly in her hands. She had no idea where that burst of courage came from, but she followed it. She wanted to be here. She wanted to he *his*.

His tongue flicked over her pearl again. She hissed through her teeth, gripping at his hair more tightly. She found herself stretching her legs, pulling him closer, keeping him there, all so he could give her more.

"Mmmm..." she heard him say, and immediately after, he took her into his whole mouth.

It was a sensation unlike anything she had ever felt before. The wet warmth of his mouth enveloped her, but instead of being pleasured and satiated, she kept wanting more and more. There was never enough of his tongue, of his presence, of his touch.

His tongue continued licking her, teasing her, parting her folds, then sliding inside of her. Everything about the sight of him between her legs drove her mad, madder than she had ever been. Her hips bucked against his face, yearning for more, even as he gave her all she wanted.

She rocked against his mouth, feeling a sudden tidal wave of pleasure. Her entire body clenched, and that was when she lost control. Her fingers held him in place, his tongue having sunk deep inside of her. She moaned loudly, closing her eyes, allowing ecstasy to wash over her.

When she opened her eyes, she was still trembling. His lips were still wet, and she felt a desire to kiss him, but the need to watch him was overpowering. It was as if he might disappear if she looked away even for a single moment.

Gently, he lowered the hem of her gown, and now, save for her flushed cheeks, it was as if nothing had happened. He got up, wiping his lips with his thumb, but there was a flicker of a smile there, as he reverently placed the book back in its place.

His eyes darkened as he watched her. "Such poetry, Charlotte, is what can ruin a good man."

Chapter Sixteen

Charlotte had tried, all morning, to read.

The book lay open on her lap, the words as indistinct as smoke. She had turned three pages and absorbed not a single line. Every thought, every breath, seemed to circle back to Cassian and the way his voice had wrapped around the verses he read, until the air itself seemed to tremble.

It had been three days since that moment, yet the memory lingered with unsettling vividness. She pressed a hand to her breast as if to quiet her heartbeat. How foolish she was, how hopelessly eager to give herself to him.

At night, the thought of him would not leave her. The memory of his nearness, the warmth that had spread through her as he pleasured her... it haunted her like a fever. She would lie awake long after the lamps were extinguished, caught between shame and longing, between what she had been taught to feel and what her body insisted upon remembering.

It was unbearable, and yet she could not wish it away.

At last, she shut the book and rose. The air in her room felt stifling. She needed movement and fresh air, something to quiet the restless tide within her.

Her maid, Miriam, looked up as she reached for her cloak. "Your Grace? Shall I fetch the carriage?"

"No," Charlotte said quickly. "It is only a short errand. I wish to walk."

"But the weather—"

"It will hold."

She forced a smile, though her heart was pounding with a strange, reckless energy. For the first time since her marriage, she felt an almost desperate need to step outside her as the Duchess of Duskbourne, as the woman trapped between pride and desire, and simply be herself.

"Begging your pardon, Your Grace, but the Duke would not like you to go alone. He'd have my position for it."

Charlotte gave a soft, indulgent laugh, stepping closer. "My dear Miriam, do you imagine I'm about to elope in the middle of the morning?"

Miriam's eyes widened. "No, of course not—"

"Then you've nothing to fear." Charlotte smiled, gently brushing the girl's sleeve. "It's only to Lydia's shop, you know it. I've been there a hundred times."

"But His Grace—"

"Will never know," Charlotte interrupted softly. "Unless you mean to tell him?"

Miriam blinked, flustered. "I'd never, Your Grace."

"Then there's no harm done." Charlotte took up her gloves and leaned in just a touch, lowering her voice to a conspiratorial murmur. "Besides, you'd only catch cold standing about while I speak with Lydia about muslin and stitching. Imagine the boredom."

Miriam's stern expression faltered, while her mouth twitched in reluctant amusement. "You're very persuasive, Your Grace."

"I try," Charlotte said sweetly. "And I shall return before luncheon. If anyone asks, I am resting with a book and wish not to be disturbed."

Miriam sighed in defeat. "Very well. But if anyone should notice—"

"They won't." Charlotte drew up her hood and smiled radiantly. "You have my word."

The air outside was brisk and alive. Each step along the gravel path felt like an unspoken rebellion, her pulse quickening with every turn of the road away from Duskbourne. For once, she was neither duchess nor wife, only herself.

For a time, she allowed herself to breathe and to relish the quiet. But after a few streets, a strange awareness crept upon her. She could feel a presence behind her and hear the faint rhythm of another's footsteps matching her own.

She slowed. The sound slowed, too.

A chill pricked at the back of her neck. She turned, expecting to see some villager, perhaps a boy running errands, but the street was nearly empty. Only a cart creaked in the distance, and a thin mist lingered above the rooftops.

She told herself she was being foolish and continued on.

Yet no sooner had she turned the next corner than a figure stepped suddenly into her path.

"Charlotte."

She was startled by her name being spoken so softly, almost reverently. It made her freeze, all the more so when she realized to whom the voice belonged.

Edmund Larke looked very much as she remembered him, though now he appeared thinner and paler. His eyes shone with that same self-satisfied light that once might have seemed so poetic, but which now struck her as feverish.

He removed his hat with a flourish. "I can scarcely believe it. To see you, *truly* see you, after all this time."

Charlotte's heart lurched, but she drew herself up. "Mr. Larke. You should not be here."

"I had to be," he said fervently. "When I learned who you'd become... I thought my heart would break. But fate has given me this moment. Surely you feel it too?"

"I feel only astonishment at your audacity," she said sharply. "I heard what you told your friends about me, all those horrible words about my emotions for you."

He raised an eyebrow. "You... were there?"

"I was," she said, evidently catching him off guard. "And now, you presume to address me after what you did?"

"Charlotte, please." He took a step forward, but his expression of wounded pride was too theatrical. "You must believe me, my intentions were never as base as you think. I was desperate, misled, undone by circumstance—"

"You were deceitful," she interrupted him. "You courted me for my fortune and spoke of love as if it were currency. Whatever desperation you claim, it does not excuse deceit."

Edmund's face twitched. His charm was already faltering. "You misunderstand. I loved you then, and I love you still. Surely you cannot have forgotten what we shared... those letters, those words—"

"Words," she said bitterly. "That was all you ever had. And now, even they ring hollow."

He reached for her hand suddenly. "Charlotte, I beg you—"

She recoiled. "Do not touch me."

"Only listen," he implored, grasping her wrist before she could step back. "I know I wronged you, but I can make it right. Leave him, that cold, joyless man, and come with me. You were never meant to live behind stone walls and formality—"

"Release me at once." Her voice rose, clear and cutting.

Before Edmund could reply, another voice came from behind them.

"Unhand her."

Edmund froze. Charlotte turned, and her breath caught. Cassian stood a few paces away, his expression thunderous. His dark coat and gloves were immaculate, and his stance composed, but despite all that, the fury in his eyes was unmistakable.

"Who are you?" Cassian demanded. "And why do you presume to lay hands upon my wife?"

"Your Grace," Edmund stammered, releasing her wrist at once. "This is a misunderstanding... I merely wished to—"

"I asked you a question," Cassian snarled.

Edmund faltered under the weight of his gaze. "I—I meant no harm. An old acquaintance, nothing more."

"Acquaintance?" Cassian's eyes flicked briefly to Charlotte, then back to Edmund. "You will leave this place now, Mr.—?"

"Larke. Edmund Larke, sir."

Cassian's mouth tightened. "Then leave, Mr. Larke, before I make certain your name is not spoken in any respectable drawing room in London ever again."

The colour drained from Edmund's face. He bowed stiffly, muttered something that might have been an apology, and retreated down the street with his back hunched.

That was when Charlotte's composure faltered. The shock of Edmund's sudden appearance and the memory of his hand on her wrist hit her all at once. Her breath caught, sharp and uneven.

Cassian noticed immediately. Without a word, he hurried toward her, and before she could protest, he drew her into his arms.

It was not a gentle embrace, nor a hesitant one. It was firm, steady, a containment of trembling energy. She stiffened for a heartbeat, startled by the suddenness of it, then let herself sink into the strength of him. His coat was cold from the wind, but beneath it she could feel the steady rhythm of his heartbeat.

"Charlotte," he said quietly, his breath brushing against her hair. "You're safe now."

She closed her eyes.

For a moment, she could only stand there, listening to that low voice that carried authority and something dangerously close to tenderness. His arm tightened, and the rest of the world seemed to fall away.

"I am sorry," she whispered. "He startled me."

Cassian's jaw tightened. "You need not apologize for another man's impropriety."

She drew back enough to look at him, to drink in the sight of him. "You frightened him away."

"Good," he said curtly. "I only wish I had arrived sooner."

His hand lingered at the small of her back, steadying her. "You are safe," he said again. "You do not need to worry when I am here."

Something in his tone made her chest tighten. It was more than reassurance. It was a promise. It was possession, and perhaps even confession, all at once.

When she had steadied herself, he offered his arm again. "Come," he said. "We're going home."

She nodded, too tired to argue. The walk back passed in silence, though the warmth of his hand at her elbow seemed to burn through her cloak.

***

At Duskbourne, the butler opened the door before they reached it. Cassian said nothing. He merely guided Charlotte through the hall and toward his study. When the door closed behind them, the quiet was almost deafening.

Cassian turned to face her. "Sit, please."

She obeyed, though she sensed what was coming.

He paced once before the hearth, then faced her. "I will ask you this only once, Charlotte. Why were you walking in the village without a chaperone?"

"I needed air," she replied.

"Duskbourne has gardens enough for that."

"I wanted to see Lydia."

"Then you should have taken Miriam with you. Or the carriage. Or both."

Her spine straightened. "Must every step I take be watched and accounted for?"

"When you are my wife," he said sharply, "your safety is my concern."

"I was hardly in danger until you made it sound so."

"You *were* in danger!" he countered. "That man followed you. He could have—" He broke off, the rest lost in his clenched jaw. "Do you have any notion what might have happened had I not arrived?"

"I do," she said quietly. "I handled him before you came. I am not helpless, Cassian. You cannot keep me shut away in this house like one of your ledgers and have me ordered, accounted for, and perfectly contained."

His eyes narrowed, that muscle in his jaw ticking again. "You mistake protection for confinement."

"And you mistake control for care," she shot back.

He stared her down, inhaling through his teeth. He looked like he was about to shout or run away, or both at the same time. But he did neither.

Instead, he strode over to her in a single second and gripped her by the waist with both hands. Before she had any idea what was happening, she was seated on his writing table, with him kneeling before her and her gown already pooled around her waist.

She knew that she shouldn't have given in with such ease. But how could she say anything when she knew what was coming?

Her irritation with him was kissed away by his lips as if it were never there. His tongue was licking her most intimate flesh all over again, just like the last time, and all she could do was give in. Just a few languid licks were enough for her to sell her soul to this man. And she would have done it gladly all over again.

"Oh..." she moaned, closing her eyes, once again gripping his hair to keep him in place, as if he might change his mind and leave.

She could feel his tongue stretching her, delving deeper, and she knew she was close. He had brought her to the edge even faster than last time.

And just as she was about to explode into nothingness, he suddenly pulled away.

She gasped silently, watching him with her eyes wide open. She expected him to continue, to go back down to his knees, but he simply grinned at her and pulled away, leaving her raw and exposed.

"What..." she started, but she couldn't finish the thought when her entire body yearned for the release that had been stolen from her.

"No," he said, shaking his head as well as his index finger at her. "You were a naughty girl. And naughty girls don't get what they want."

Without waiting for her to say anything, he paraded toward the door and closed it behind him, leaving her hot, bothered, and utterly mad with both rage and desire.

Chapter Seventeen

The morning found Cassian in his office at the manufactory, a space far removed from the austere quiet of Duskbourne Hall. The low hum of conversation from the adjoining rooms and the faint hiss of steam and machinery beyond the walls were the sort of activity that steadied him.

Here, things were measurable: numbers, contracts, yields, and profits. There was no emotion and no Charlotte.

Gideon entered without knocking, as usual.

"Well, Duskbourne," he drawled, tossing his gloves onto a chair, "I must say, marriage appears to suit you. There's a distinct improvement in your temper. You've gone an entire month without threatening to throttle a member of Parliament."

Cassian looked up from the ledger before him. "An oversight I intend to correct before the quarter's end."

Gideon laughed, settling into the chair opposite. "You may posture all you like, but you've that unmistakable look of a man recently domestic. Polished boots, no missed appointments, and," his gaze sharpened slightly, amused, "a certain distracted air that can only mean your duchess is occupying more of your mind than you'll admit."

Cassian's quill stilled, though his tone remained even. "I am occupied, Harrow, with business, not sentiment."

"If you say so," Gideon murmured, clearly unconvinced. "Though between us, I'd wager your wife is far more interesting than balance sheets."

Cassian gave him a level look. "Balance sheets, at least, do not argue."

Gideon laughed outright. "Ah, so the domestic calm is not so calm after all."

Cassian ignored him, closing the ledger and setting it aside. "We'll discuss your delight in my private affairs another time. I expect Hawthorne shortly. We have matters to resolve before the week is out."

At the mention of Charlotte's brother, Gideon's grin faded into a look of mild wariness. "The Duke of Hawthorne. Sensible fellow, though I can't imagine he finds you an easy ally."

"Nor I him," Cassian said dryly. "But we share an interest in keeping the textile venture solvent. It will do."

A knock at the door interrupted them. The clerk ushered Nicholas Montclair inside. He had the wary air of a man who distrusted most people by principle and Cassian Oberon by habit.

"Hawthorne," Cassian greeted.

"Duskbourne," Nicholas replied, bowing slightly before taking a seat. His gaze swept the office. "Mr. Harrow."

"Your Grace," Gideon said amiably. "Good of you to join our humble conclave of ambition."

Nicholas gave him a look that managed to convey both civility and mild disdain. "I hear we are to discuss expansion."

"Indeed." Cassian inclined his head toward the map spread across the table. "Local production has stabilized. The Grantham mills are operating at full capacity, and your wife's venture has drawn respectable profit. The question before us is whether we mean to remain provincial or become something larger."

Nicholas's expression sharpened. "Lydia is cautious about overextending too soon."

"As she should be," Cassian agreed. "But I have cousins in the Low Countries, Rotterdam and Antwerp, and they handle trade in linen and wool. They have connections among the merchants there. If we wish to export our textiles, it would be prudent to use a channel we can trust."

Gideon leaned forward. "An excellent notion. There's demand abroad for English fabrics, especially when they're of quality. With your family's connections, Duskbourne, we could secure distribution before anyone else catches wind of it."

Nicholas regarded him steadily. "Trade abroad is no small risk. I'd prefer assurances that your cousins' interests do not conflict with ours."

Cassian's tone cooled slightly. "My family's reputation is not for dishonour."

"Reputation," Nicholas returned evenly, "is not the same as proof."

The room stilled. Gideon, ever the peacemaker, interjected smoothly.

"Gentlemen, let us assume everyone here values both profit *and* family honour. The figures speak for themselves. If managed properly, this venture could double the current yield within the year."

Cassian exhaled slowly, mastering his irritation. "My proposal is simple. We send a test shipment, small, contained, through a single partner. If it succeeds, we expand. If not, we withdraw."

Nicholas considered this, then nodded once. "A cautious approach. Very well."

They continued to speak of tariffs and shipment routes, their dialogue as dry as the parchment before them. Gideon, with his usual charm, steered the conversation when it risked dissolving into silence, but it was clear that Hawthorne had come less to negotiate than to assess.

And somewhere amid talk of duties and export permits, the mood began to shift. Cassian mentioned the terrain surrounding one of his mills, namely the difficulty of carting goods across rough ground, and how he'd thought to clear a small portion of the land for a smoother route.

Nicholas looked up, interest flickering across his usually impassive face. "The western lands? I've ridden it. Excellent ground for game once the season begins. Have you considered letting some of it?"

Cassian's mouth curved faintly. "I have. Though the last tenant left the area in disrepair. I've been overseeing the restoration myself."

"A duke, overseeing fieldwork," Nicholas said with a hint of wry amusement. "That must astonish your peers in London."

"I find astonishment an excellent deterrent against interference," Cassian replied.

To his mild surprise, Nicholas laughed.

From there, the conversation lightened. They spoke of acreage, soil composition, even of horses. They talked of Cassian's stallion from his northern stud and Nicholas's prized hunter bred from the same lineage. Their shared appreciation for precision in figures, in breeding, and in planning revealed itself gradually, like two players discovering they favoured the same strategy on opposite sides of a chessboard. By the time they reached an agreement on the terms of export, the air between them had eased noticeably.

"Well," Nicholas said, closing the ledger, "I must admit, Duskbourne, you are not so impossible as I'd imagined."

"I shall endeavour to maintain the illusion," Cassian replied, allowing the faintest glint of humour to show.

Even Gideon looked mildly astonished. "I never thought I'd live to see the day you two spoke without needing a referee."

Nicholas gave a small smile, rising from his chair. "My sister's influence, perhaps."

At that, Cassian's expression sobered. He stood as well, with his hands resting lightly on the table. "Hawthorne..." He hesitated, then said more quietly, "May I speak plainly?"

Nicholas inclined his head. "Of course."

"I know you have reason to... question me," Cassian began, feeling strangely nervous. "And I would not fault you for it. But I want you to know that I will not harm your sister. You have my word."

Nicholas regarded him in silence for a long moment. His eyes, so like Charlotte's, were steady and searching.

"I believe you," he said finally. "You strike me as a man who does not make vows lightly."

"I do not."

Nicholas nodded once, looking satisfied. "Then we shall get along well enough."

They shook hands in a brief, firm clasp, the kind that did not seal friendship yet, but perhaps the beginning of respect.

When Nicholas and Gideon had departed, Cassian remained by the window, looking out across the yard where carriages waited in neat rows. The sunlight gleamed off their polished sides, dazzling and cold.

He had meant what he said. He would never hurt Charlotte. Of that, he was certain. But he had promised not to wound her body, and what of her heart?

He had never learned how to love without breaking something. And as much as he tried to deny it, he feared that if he ever let himself love her fully, it would destroy them both.

***

Cassian returned to Duskbourne that afternoon with the distinct satisfaction of a man who had survived both negotiation and diplomacy without throttling anyone. It was, he reflected, no small victory.

He handed his gloves to the butler and was just loosening his cravat when he heard quick, familiar footsteps in the corridor.

Charlotte appeared, bright-eyed and breathless, with a folded letter in hand. "You look remarkably intact for a man who has spent the day in meetings."

He arched a brow. "You sound disappointed."

"Not disappointed," she said with a teasing tilt of her head. "Only surprised. Nicholas has been known to leave men pale and trembling."

"He restrained himself," Cassian replied dryly. "Though I suspect your brother measures civility by the teaspoon."

Her lips curved. "Then you must have impressed him."

He paused, studying her expression, because he noticed the mischief there, the spark he both admired and dreaded. "I'll take that as a compliment."

"Good, because it was one," she said, stepping closer and holding out the letter. "We've received an invitation to the Cavendish Charity Ball."

Cassian took the envelope, skimming through it briefly. "I see. The usual parade of vanity and artifice."

"Also known as the pinnacle of the Season," she reminded him. "Half of London will be there. It's rather an honour, you know."

"I was unaware we sought honours," he murmured.

"You may not be, Your Grace," she replied playfully, "but your duchess is growing rather weary of being thought a recluse."

He glanced up sharply at that, but she smiled innocently. "We must attend, of course. Appearances, as you so often remind me, must be preserved."

"Indeed," he said, returning the letter to her. "We shall attend. You will have your moment of spectacle."

"Splendid." She slipped the invitation into her pocket, then looked up at him with a glint of daring. "Though I must warn you... You'll need to dance."

He gave her a flat look. "I do not dance."

"You *can't* dance, you mean?"

"I mean that I *choose* not to," he said evenly.

"Because you dislike being touched?" she asked, her tone deceptively light.

The question hit its mark. Cassian's jaw tightened. "Because I dislike meaningless displays."

"Then perhaps you should give it meaning," she murmured.

He blinked, taken aback by her audacity. Charlotte, seeming to sense her advantage, smiled. Then, she took a step closer.

"Besides," she continued, sounding seductive, "I should like to see whether your legendary composure holds when you're surrounded by people and music and the eyes of everyone watching."

He stared down at her, feeling his every muscle taut. "You enjoy provoking me."

"A little," she admitted, and her lovely lips looked more kissable than ever as she smiled at him. "It seems to be the only way to make you feel *alive.*"

He exhaled a short, dangerous laugh. "And what precisely do you imagine you'll achieve by teasing me in the middle of the corridor?"

"Perhaps nothing," she said, her gaze dangerously steady on his. "Perhaps everything."

She was even closer now. In fact, she was close enough that the faint scent of her skin tangled with his thoughts. Her fingers brushed the edge of his sleeve, an innocent touch made incendiary by circumstance.

"Charlotte..." he said softly, warningly.

"Yes, Your Grace?" she replied with a voice as sweet as honey. "Why, we are only talking, nothing else."

He didn't move. To be quite honest, he didn't dare to. The hall was open and any servant could walk by, yet he found himself entirely unable to step back. His pulse thrummed in his throat.

She tilted her head, and there was a victorious smile on her lips. She knew *exactly* what she was doing.

Then, with graceful calm, she stepped back, smoothed her skirts, and said brightly. "Then it's settled. We shall attend the ball."

He blinked, as if waking from a spell. "You are incorrigible."

"I've been called worse," she said over her shoulder, glancing back once as she walked away. "Don't be late for supper, Cassian."

He watched her go and let out a slow breath he hadn't realized he'd been holding.

Damn her.

She had left him standing in his own corridor, with his heart pounding like a schoolboy's. For the first time in years, Cassian Oberon, the Duke of Duskbourne, had no idea whether he wished to strangle his wife or kiss her senseless.

Chapter Eighteen

The morning began in its usual order, following clear skies, punctual clerks, and the quiet hum of industry that always steadied Cassian's mind. By the time he reached his office with Gideon in tow, he had half convinced himself that the disquiet Charlotte had stirred the night before had been a fleeting distraction, easily mastered.

That illusion lasted all of ten minutes.

"Something's wrong," the head clerk stammered, pale beneath his powdered wig as Cassian entered.

Cassian set down his gloves. "Define *wrong*."

"The shipment from Leeds, Your Grace. It hasn't arrived. The ledger shows it dispatched three days ago, but there's been no receipt, and the carrier reports no sign of it along the northern road."

Cassian's expression didn't change, but a faint pulse ticked in his jaw. "You've confirmed the route? Spoke to the foreman?"

"Yes, Your Grace. Twice. No record. No crates, no bill of landing, nothing."

"*Nothing*," Cassian repeated with razor-sharp focus. "And when were you planning to inform me?"

"This morning, Your Grace. As soon as we knew it was no mere delay."

Gideon, who had been leaning against the doorframe, straightened. "What was in the shipment?"

"Documents," Cassian said grimly, "and finished textiles from the northern mill, samples for our overseas partners. If they've gone missing, every negotiation with Antwerp will collapse before it begins."

"Could it be theft?" Gideon asked.

"Perhaps... or incompetence." Cassian's gaze flicked to the clerk, who swallowed hard. "Either way, it will cost us dearly. The merchants will not wait. They will find another supplier by week's end."

He crossed to his desk, listening to the sound of papers rustling as he searched through the correspondence. There was no letter, no receipt, no explanation. Each missing piece of information was like a blow against his composure.

Gideon tried for levity. "You've weathered worse storms, Cassian. It's business, not battle."

Cassian did not look up. "For men whose names are not bound to every enterprise they touch, perhaps."

His hand came down flat upon the desk, the sound echoing sharply in the room. "This was my responsibility. I vouched for the security of those goods. If the shipment's lost, I am made to look negligent, and Duskbourne's word means less than a tradesman's."

"Steady on," Gideon murmured, though his eyes had grown serious.

But Cassian was already pacing. The office was usually his place of order and reason, but now, it suddenly seemed too small.

"Check every record," he said to the clerk. "Speak to the Leeds carrier again. Find the driver, the overseer, the warehouse keeper, every man who touched those crates."

"Yes, Your Grace." The clerk hurried out.

When the door closed, Gideon crossed to the window, watching him. "You'll drive yourself to exhaustion at this rate."

"I'll do what is necessary," Cassian said curtly.

"Ah," Gideon murmured. "There it is. The famous Duskbourne creed."

Cassian shot him a look. "If I fail in business, I fail my tenants, my workers, *everyone* who depends upon me. Failure is not an indulgence I can afford."

Gideon regarded him for a long moment, then said quietly. "It's not failure that worries me, Cassian. It's the way you punish yourself for what you cannot control."

Cassian turned away, rubbing his jaw. "There is nothing I cannot control."

But even as he said it, the words rang hollow. The truth was that he had felt out of control for days; ever since Charlotte had begun to unsettle him in ways no man, no market, no ledger ever had. And now, with this disaster threatening his reputation, the fragile order he clung to was beginning to splinter.

He feared that he was losing control of his life once again, as had happened with Eleanor. He'd been powerless to save her, just like he'd been powerless to save their child. Now, that same sensation was threatening to take over his life.

He sank into his chair, staring at the blank space on his desk where the missing documents ought to have been. His temples throbbed under the weight of responsibility.

Somewhere in the back of his mind, Charlotte's voice echoed, light, teasing, and infuriatingly alive: *You mistake control for care.*

He exhaled slowly, forcing the thought away. Charlotte had no business haunting him here.

***

By the time Cassian reached Duskbourne, the sun had already dipped behind the trees, and the wind carried a bite of coming rain. The journey home had done little to cool his temper.

Every mile had turned his thoughts tighter: missing shipments, misplaced documents, the unrelenting incompetence of others. It wasn't merely irritation. No. It was the gnawing fear of disorder, of losing control.

He handed his hat and coat to the butler with as few words as necessary and strode toward his study, intent on solitude. But solitude, it seemed, was not to be granted.

Charlotte appeared at the end of the corridor, holding a small bundle of correspondence.

"Cassian," she greeted him in a tone that was bright but still cautious. "You're late. I thought you might have stayed to dine with Gideon."

"I had no appetite for company," he said shortly, moving past her.

She turned, keeping pace beside him. "Did the meeting not go well?"

He exhaled sharply through his nose. "The meeting was tolerable. Everything else was not."

"May I ask what happened?"

"Business happened."

Her brow furrowed. "That is not an answer."

"No," he snapped, halting. "But it is all I intend to give."

Charlotte blinked, taken aback by his tone. "I beg your pardon—"

"You are not required to beg anything," he cut in. As he spoke, he could hear his voice, too sharp and too cold, but he could do nothing to change it. "But neither must you question me about matters you cannot possibly understand."

Her spine straightened. "Matters I cannot understand?" she repeated softly. "I see."

He dragged a hand through his hair, already regretting the words, but pride kept him silent.

Charlotte's eyes flashed. "I am not one of your clerks to be dismissed when inconvenient. If you are angry, say so, but do not take it out upon me."

"I am not angry with you," he said through his teeth.

"Then perhaps you should learn the difference between anger and cruelty," she shot back.

The words struck like a slap, not because they were false, but because they were painfully near the truth.

"Charlotte," he said after a moment.

"No," she said, stepping closer. "You cannot hide behind that tone forever, as though authority were a shield. You snap, you glower, and you retreat, and then wonder why the world fears to come near you!"

"Better that than to invite chaos," he returned.

"Is that what you think I am?"

Her voice was soft now, trembling not with fear but with fury and a quiet, contained blaze that made something in him twist.

He met her gaze without flinching. "You are many things, Charlotte. Predictable is not among them."

Her eyes searched his face. "And you... you are afraid to be anything *but* predictable."

Silence fell between them, sharp as glass.

He saw the pulse at her throat and the rise and fall of her breath. The defiant glint in her blue eyes undid him. He wanted to pull her close and silence her with his mouth. But the anger in him and the shame of his own temper made the thought unbearable.

She shook her head, choosing to speak, because she obviously realized he would not. "You cannot control everything, Cassian. Not in business. Not in life. And certainly not me."

He turned away before she could see the muscle working in his jaw. "Go to bed, Charlotte."

"I will," she said evenly, "when I choose to."

And with that, she swept past him. Her skirts brushed against his hand. Whether it was by accident or done on purpose, he could not tell. But still, it was a fleeting, maddening whisper of touch that lingered long after she was gone.

Cassian stood motionless in the dim corridor, feeling his pulse thundering in his ears.

All he had ever wanted was to preserve order, because that was the only way to keep the world from unravelling. But somehow, every word he spoke to her seemed to hasten the undoing.

At last, he made his way to the study, poured himself a glass of brandy, and stared into the fire. A second glass followed the first. He sat down in his chair, his elbows on his knees, staring at the flames until they blurred. His mind, despite every effort, would not quiet.

He thought of *her*.

No woman had ever looked at him like that, in such a manner that was unafraid, unyielding, as though she could see the man beneath the title and found him wanting.

He should have been angry still. He *was* angry at her for defying him, at himself for provoking her. But anger was a poor disguise for what churned beneath. It was desire: raw, unbidden, and growing harder to ignore with each passing day.

He remembered the first time she had defied him with words sharp enough to draw blood. He remembered how her cheeks had flushed; how bright her eyes were. How easily her temper matched his, and how he'd wanted, absurdly, to taste that fire rather than extinguish it.

The memory of their kiss, of him tasting her in those furious, shattering moments of madness, struck him with such clarity that his hand tightened around the glass. The heat of her mouth, the tremor in her breath, the feel of her body pressed to his... it all returned with cruel precision.

He had told himself it meant nothing. That it was anger, not longing. That she had provoked him, and he'd only sought to silence her. But it was a lie, and one he could no longer sustain.

She had become a constant in his thoughts, uninvited and unstoppable.

He set the glass down too roughly, and the sound exploded sharply against the quiet.

"Fool," he muttered under his breath.

Passion had cost him once before. It had taken everything he loved. He would not make that mistake again.

He leaned back, pressing a hand to his brow. The image of his late wife came unbidden to him. Just like he had promised Charlotte, he made the same promise to Eleanor: all would be well. What was worse, he believed it.

What arrogance.

If he had only waited before trying for a child, if only he had seen how frail Eleanor was becoming, instead of trusting blindly and foolishly that all would be well. He felt the same thing happening now. He was trusting fate without any reason to do so.

He exhaled slowly, but the air caught in his throat. The study blurred for a moment before he forced the emotion back into its cage.

"Enough," he muttered to an empty room, as though he could command his thoughts.

But his mind would not obey. Love had cost Eleanor her life. It cost him everything that mattered. What right had he to want again? To hope again?

He had proven what his affection brought: destruction and grief.

Chapter Nineteen

The letter arrived in the late morning, nestled among invitations, charitable correspondence, and a note from Lydia regarding the upcoming Cavendish Ball. Charlotte might have overlooked it entirely had she not recognized that same sweeping, self-important script that turned her stomach the instant she saw it.

She should have burned it at once, as she had the last one. But once again, curiosity got the better of her and forced her fingers to break the seal.

My Dearest Charlotte,

I had hoped my earlier letter would soften your heart, but your silence has wounded me more deeply than you can imagine. Still, I am not without compassion. I understand your position with the ducal husband and the appearances you must maintain.

Yet I cannot accept that you would throw away what we shared. You once loved me, Charlotte, and love cannot be so easily buried beneath title and silk. If you refuse to meet me, I may be driven to less pleasant measures, for it would grieve me to see your reputation suffer, and your husband learn that his duchess once wrote letters of a most tender nature to another man.

Yours, in love and in resolve,

E.L.

Charlotte's hand trembled as she reached the final line, though not from fear alone.

The nerve of him. The audacity!

To write to her again, after all his lies and worse! To threaten her with scandal! The letter felt like a stain against her fingers.

She rose abruptly and crossed the room, pacing the carpet with quick, controlled steps. Her mind moved faster than her breath, darting through every consequence: what Cassian would say if he found out, or how the ton would whisper if Edmund dared follow through.

A single malicious sentence could destroy everything she had rebuilt so far. But then another thought cut through the panic.

No. He will not ruin me again.

Whatever Edmund imagined, he no longer held power over her. She had survived humiliation once. She would not surrender to fear a second time. She went to the fire and stood there for a long while, watching the flames twist and flicker. Her first instinct was to burn the letter, but she hesitated. Perhaps it would be wiser to keep it. Proof, should Edmund's threats ever reach another's ears.

With a deep breath, she folded it neatly and slipped it into the drawer beneath her writing desk, locking it away.

By noon, Charlotte resolved to think no more of Edmund Larke.

He had stolen enough of her peace once, and she would not let him do so again. With the letter safely locked away, she summoned her carriage.

Lydia had written the previous day to say the final fitting for Charlotte's gown was ready, the same gown she was to wear at the Cavendish Ball. A trifle of fashion, perhaps, but after the morning's dark agitation, the idea of lace and colour and easy conversation seemed like a balm.

The moment she stepped into *Grantham & Co. Fine Textiles,* the scent of starch and silk enveloped her. Lydia's laughter could be heard even before she appeared.

"Charlotte!" Lydia cried, coming forward with a pin cushion still strapped to her wrist. "You've arrived just in time, my dear. I was about to send word to Duskbourne. Come, you must see it."

Charlotte smiled, shedding her cloak. "You sound as though you've discovered buried treasure."

"In a way, I have." Lydia motioned her toward the fitting room. "Wait until you see what we've made of that dove-grey silk."

The gown awaited her on a dress form. It was a pale silver-grey with the softest shimmer, and its embroidery was delicate and precise. The fabric caught the light with every movement, gleaming faintly blue in the shadows. A sweep of gossamer lace framed the neckline, and the waist was drawn perfectly to flatter her figure.

Charlotte stood silent for a moment. "Oh," she breathed at last. "Lydia, it's... beautiful."

"I should hope so," Lydia said with mock severity. "It took three nights and more than one argument with my tailor to achieve that shade. But come, try it on. You cannot judge a gown until it breathes with the woman wearing it."

Charlotte laughed softly and allowed herself to be ushered behind the screen.

When she emerged, Lydia let out a low whistle. "Well, look at you! If the duke doesn't fall properly in love with you at the Cavendish Ball, I shall lose faith in all men entirely."

"Don't be absurd," Charlotte said, though warmth rose in her cheeks.

"Absurd?" Lydia circled her, appraising the fit. "My dear, you look like moonlight made flesh. That colour was born for you."

Charlotte turned toward the looking glass, and for what seemed to be an eternity, she simply gazed at herself. The reflection staring back did not resemble the quiet, cautious woman she had been at the start of her marriage, nor the wounded, uncertain one Edmund had once deceived. The gown transformed her, yes, but so did the way she carried herself within it: poised, luminous, undeniably alive.

Her eyes met her own in the looking glass, and for the first time in what felt like years, she saw not a woman diminished by the past, but one defined by her own choices.

"I had forgotten," she said quietly, "what it felt like to be..." She hesitated.

Lydia's tone softened. "Seen?"

Charlotte smiled faintly. "Yes."

Lydia rested a hand on her shoulder. "Well, then. Let them all see, my dear. Every last one of them."

Charlotte's reflection smiled back with quiet certainty. Whatever awaited her at the Cavendish Ball, be it gossip, scrutiny, or Cassian's unreadable gaze, she would face it with her head held high.

She spent another hour in Lydia's company, then headed back home, with the gown carefully folded in its box, feeling some fragile return to confidence.

By the time she reached the house, twilight had begun to fall, painting the windows in rose and gold. She handed her cloak to Miriam and was halfway to her room when the butler stopped her.

"Your Grace," he said, offering a small tray. "A letter was delivered for you not half an hour ago."

She froze.

Another letter.

Her heart sank even before she saw the handwriting. For a moment, she could not bring herself to touch it. The earlier defiance she had felt gave way to a dull, cold dread. He had written again, despite her silence.

Meet me or I will reveal everything.

The threat seemed to echo before she even opened the envelope. She broke the seal with trembling fingers, going over the lines in growing horror.

You yourself force me to do this, Charlotte. I had hoped you might see reason, but your silence leaves me no choice. If you will not meet me, I shall deliver your letters, those sweet tokens of devotion you once wrote, directly into the hands of your husband. You know what scandal will follow.

Meet me at the old oak by the crossroads on Thursday at noon, or I will take it as your answer that I must act otherwise.

You can still prevent all of this.

E.L.

Her breath caught. The words blurred before her eyes, and she pressed a hand to her mouth, steadying herself. For one unguarded moment, fear broke through her composure.

"Charlotte?"

She turned sharply.

Cassian stood at the end of the corridor, half-shadowed by the fading light. His eyes moved from her face to the letter in her hand.

"What is that?"

"It's nothing," she said quickly, folding the page.

His gaze hardened. "*Nothing* seldom looks like that."

She hesitated, then said quietly. "A private matter, nothing for you to be concerned about."

"From whom?"

Her silence was answer enough.

Cassian's voice dropped dangerously low. "Is it from *him*?"

She flinched.

He took a step closer. "I see." His tone was calm, but it was the calm before a storm. "I thought that business with your poet was finished."

"It is," she replied, too hastily.

"Evidently not." His eyes, usually so controlled, burned with something darker now. He seemed to be not only angry, but also hurt. "You've been receiving his letters, and you said nothing."

"I had no reason to burden you with it."

"No reason?" His voice sharpened. "You conceal letters from another man, a man you once—" He stopped short, gritting his teeth.

She felt her temper flare despite the sick ache in her chest. "Do not finish that sentence."

"You expect me to stand by while he writes to you, threatens you, perhaps still—"

"Cassian, enough!"

Her cry rang through the hall. For a long moment, neither of them spoke. The air between them crackled with fury and pain, and neither was able to control it.

Then she spoke more quietly but no less fiercely. "You think I would entertain him? After what he did? You think I would shame myself, and you, by replying to such filth?"

His eyes flicked to the letter still clutched in her hand. "I think you've hidden something from me."

"Because you would have turned it into *this*," she shot back. "Because you cannot trust anyone, not even your wife."

He flinched as if struck.

"Do you imagine," she continued, trembling now, "that I owe you blind obedience, or that my past sins have marked me unworthy of faith? I said nothing because I *rejected him*. I wanted to protect what little peace we had."

"Peace built on lies cannot last," he said coldly.

"And neither can a marriage built on suspicion."

Charlotte scarcely had time to collect her breath before Cassian moved toward her again. In that moment, she could not tell if he meant to demand or to defend.

"Show me the letter," he asked. He paused, and seeing that she didn't move, he added. "Please, Charlotte. I want to see what sort of a mad man we are truly dealing with here."

After a long pause, she surrendered it. Their fingers brushed. Hers were cold, but his were burning. Cassian unfolded the sheet and read in silence, the lines deepening at the corners of his eyes. When he finished, he said nothing. He folded the paper once, then again, as though restraining the violence of impulse.

"So, it's true," he said softly. "He *is* threatening you now."

Charlotte nodded, the tension in her throat refusing to let words pass.

"I see now." He drew a long breath. "Why didn't you tell me?"

"I was trying to sort it out on my own."

"Not with these kinds of people," he pointed out. "You should have come to me immediately."

"How could I?" she asked incredulously. "When all you do is attack?"

She saw regret in his eyes. It was plain as daylight. "I was wrong."

"You were cruel," she told him again, and she realized that word hurt him deeply.

All he could do was agree. "Yes."

For a moment, the air between them seemed flammable. Then Cassian took a step closer. "Charlotte, I—"

But she had already turned away, unable to bear the heaviness in his tone.

"Don't," she said quietly. "Please."

He reached out instinctively but let his hand fall before it touched her. She started for the door.

"Charlotte!" he called after her.

She did not stop. In two strides, he caught up with her, and his hand closed gently around her arm. It was not to restrain, but to make her pause.

"Wait," he said.

She turned, and her eyes were bright with unshed anger and hurt. "What more is there to say?"

"That I believe you," he said simply.

She stared at him, scarcely believing it.

He continued, raking his fingers through his hair. And his words were stripped of pride. "You were right. I let anger blind me. When I saw the letter, I thought only of betrayal, not of danger. But I know better now. I should have known better from the first."

Her eyes searched his face. He had never seemed this vulnerable before.

"I am sorry," he told her. "My temper is the result of some business matters gone awry, and those are in no way connected to you, but you bore the brunt of my rage."

Charlotte exhaled shakily, realizing how difficult it must have been for him to say those words. She appreciated them, but she wanted to be honest with him. "You hurt me, Cassian."

"I know." He hesitated, his grip on her arm loosening, though he did not release her entirely. "And I would sooner face a dozen scandals than hurt you again. Please, believe me."

She couldn't say anything to that. She wanted to believe him with all her heart, but her heart was a treacherous little thing.

Then, she heard him speak again. "He will not touch you again. Whatever game he plays, it ends now. Edmund Larke is dangerous, but he will not harm you or us."

The word *us* hung between them, daring them both to accept it. And all she could do was nod.

Chapter Twenty

The smell of smoke struck Cassian before the sight of flames ever reached him. His horse thundered down the last stretch of road toward the warehouse. Orange embers still glowed against the early evening sky. Men shouted orders, forming a desperate line from river to storehouse, passing bucket after bucket.

Cassian dismounted before the horse had fully stopped.

"What happened?" he demanded, striding toward the overseer.

The man, Mr. Turner, removed his cap with shaking hands. "Your Grace, the fire started inside. We... we believe it was lit on purpose."

Cassian's lungs turned to iron.

"Are you certain?" His voice remained composed, though his blood roared beneath the surface.

Turner nodded. "A barrel of oil was overturned. Someone meant for the blaze to spread. If the wind had shifted, the whole building and everything in it would've been lost."

Cassian looked to the scorched wall, which now stood blackened and cracked, and forced back the rising fury.

Sabotage. First missing shipments. Now this.

"Double the watch. No one leaves until I've spoken to them," he said. "If someone wishes to test my resolve, they will soon regret the attempt."

Before Turner could answer, a carriage rattled up the road. Cassian turned, thinking that the last thing he needed now was more distraction, but his irritation vanished when he saw

Charlotte. She stepped down from the carriage without waiting for assistance.

"Cassian!" she called, hurrying to him. "The servants said there was a fire. I came at once."

"You should not be here," he told her. She was bareheaded, breathless, and far too close to danger.

"And yet I am." She planted herself before him. "Tell me what needs doing."

"This is no place for—"

"For a duchess?" she cut in. "You forget I spent years in my brother's warehouses and Lydia's workrooms. I know how to salvage inventory, how to clear a corridor before it collapses, and how fast a cotton fire spreads. Now, either put me to use or step aside."

His retort died on his tongue. Because she was right, and because he needed every capable hand. And because he felt something fierce and unmanageable twist in his chest at the sight of her so unafraid and choosing to stand in the fire with him.

He gave one curt nod. "Very well then. Take the men on the west side. The stored fabrics and ledgers will be in that corner. Save what you can before the smoke spoils it."

Charlotte did not hesitate. She was already moving, issuing quick commands that Turner's men obeyed without question. Cassian watched as she organized them in a manner that was efficient and utterly focused. The fire fought back, flaring through broken boards, but under Charlotte's direction and Cassian's orders, the workers formed a steady rhythm. Buckets splashed. Goods were dragged to safety. Sparks died beneath wet canvas.

It took over an hour before the last of the flames surrendered.

When the smoke thinned, Cassian walked the perimeter, boots crunching over charred debris. Charlotte joined him, and he noticed a smudge of ash streaked across her cheek. He resisted the urge to wipe it gently with his thumb.

"It could have been far worse," she said softly.

"Yes." His gaze swept the wreckage. "Which is what concerns me. Someone meant to ruin us."

Us.

The word slipped out before he could catch it.

Charlotte heard it. He saw it in the way her eyes softened, like light filtering through shutters.

She touched a scorched beam. "Do you think this is connected to the missing shipment you told me about?"

He exhaled. "Possibly. Whatever this is, it is no coincidence."

Her chin lifted. "Then we face it together."

Cassian turned toward her fully. For a moment, neither spoke. The night air hummed with what had not yet been said.

"You could have been hurt," he murmured. "Running into danger like that."

"*You* were in danger," she replied simply, as though that were explanation enough.

That was when he gave in to the desire of a moment ago. He reached out, brushing his thumb across the streak of ash on her cheek. She stilled, patiently waiting, with that disarming smile on her face.

"Thank you," he said quietly. "For helping, and for not turning away."

Charlotte swallowed. "You do not always have to stand alone, Cassian."

He held her gaze for one suspended heartbeat.

"I am beginning to see that."

An hour had passed, and Cassian had just finished instructing Turner on the night watch when the sound of approaching hoofbeats drew his attention. A lone rider dismounted with an easy swing.

Gideon strode into the circle of lantern light, brushing soot from his sleeve.

"There you are," he called. "Your butler nearly fainted when I demanded to know where his duke had vanished to. I followed the smoke the rest of the way."

Cassian arched a brow. "Since when do you take evening rides for the sake of theatrics?"

"Since your household told me you were at a burning warehouse." Gideon's tone flattened. "Forgive me for assuming that required my presence."

Despite the grim setting, Cassian felt the corner of his mouth twitch, which was the closest he came to a smile. Gideon noticed and shook his head.

"I leave you alone for one night, and everything catches fire," he muttered. "Now tell me what in God's name happened."

Cassian briefed him on the oil and the deliberate placement. Gideon listened with arms crossed, his expression growing darker by the minute.

When Cassian finished, Gideon exhaled through his teeth. "So we are certainly dealing with sabotage. The question becomes: who profits from crippling your warehouses and shipments?"

"Competitors," Cassian answered. "Political adversaries. Men who would prefer I stay silent in Parliament. Or" his jaw tightened, "someone with a more personal motive."

Gideon glanced toward Charlotte, who stood a few paces away, speaking softly with two workers as they catalogued what goods might be salvaged. Soot marked her gown. Her hair had loosened from its pins. Yet she looked composed and steadier than half his men.

"Your duchess," Gideon said under his breath, "is handling this better than most generals I know."

Cassian did not deny it. "She saved a third of the stock," he replied quietly. "And she kept the men from panicking. Without her, the loss would be twice as great."

Gideon's gaze slid back to him. "You say that as though it astonishes you."

Cassian hesitated. "It does not astonish me," he said at last. "But I... have long been unaccustomed to relying on another."

Gideon's expression softened with rare seriousness. "Then it is fortunate she gives you reason to reconsider."

Before Cassian could respond, Charlotte returned to them, brushing ash from her sleeves.

"We've secured the remaining crates," she reported. "Turner will send for carpenters in the morning, but some beams must come down before then, as they're unstable. If we leave them, the whole wall may collapse."

Cassian nodded. "Agreed. We will brace them until first light. Turner!" he called. "See to it." Then, he turned to Charlotte. "What of the ledgers?"

"In my carriage," she said. "I did not want the damp to ruin the ink."

He met her gaze. "Good thinking. Thank you, Charlotte."

She blinked, surprised by the simple praise, but pleased. He could see it.

Gideon cleared his throat. "Before I am entirely forgotten, perhaps we should consider where this leaves us."

Cassian drew in a measured breath. "There are too many possibilities. I have rivals, yes, but none brazen enough to risk arson on my property. And yet, someone did. Someone either foolish... or desperate."

"We tighten security," Gideon said. "Double the guard. Move valuable stock to the manor's storage until repairs are complete."

Cassian nodded. Then, without thinking, he turned slightly toward Charlotte.

"Do you agree?"

A week ago, he would never have asked her opinion. He would have made decisions alone and expected obedience. Tonight, he found he wanted her voice in the matter.

Charlotte seemed to recognize the significance of the question. She answered carefully. "I agree with Lord Harrow. And I believe that your men must be paid extra for the night shifts. If someone is targeting you, fear will spread. Better to ensure loyalty before doubt takes root."

Cassian considered, then inclined his head. "See to it, Gideon. Double pay, beginning tonight."

Gideon's brows rose. He was obviously impressed. "As you wish."

By the time the last embers were stamped out and the beams reinforced, the moon had risen high over the warehouse. The men dispersed in weary clusters, soot-stained and exhausted, but steadier now that their duke and duchess had stood among them.

Cassian gave Turner a final instruction and shook Gideon's hand. "Thank you for coming."

Gideon smirked lightly. "What else are old friends for, if not rescuing you from flaming buildings and scandal?" His tone was wry, but his eyes were sharp. "I will return in the morning. Try not to let anything else explode before sunrise."

Cassian allowed himself to smile as he watched Gideon mount his horse and ride into the night.

Charlotte approached him. "The men will rest easier now," she said. "So should you."

He studied her in the silver wash of moonlight, with her hair loose and wind-tangled and her gown smudged with ash. She had given orders, saved goods, soothed panic, and never once faltered. He was proud of her. Proud, and something else he dared not admit, even to himself.

"We should go home," he said gently. "It has been a long night."

She nodded. Together, they began the walk back to Duskbourne. The road was quiet, broken only by the distant sounds of crickets and the rustle of wind through the fields. After a time, Charlotte spoke.

"You believe this is only the beginning."

He did not bother to deny it. "Yes."

"Then we prepare," she replied. "Together."

That word landed with force he didn't expect. But instead of being heavy around them, it nestled as if it always belonged there.

They were nearly to the estate's iron gate when Charlotte halted.

"Cassian... look."

A lone figure stood partially concealed by the hedgerow. Its silhouette was just visible against the pale gravel path. Whoever it was, they were too still to be a traveller and too bold to be a mere passerby.

Cassian stepped slightly in front of Charlotte in one instinctive motion.

"Who goes there?" he called out, without thinking.

The figure jerked, looking startled, as if it hadn't expected to be seen. Then, it fled, disappearing into the night before Cassian could pursue.

Charlotte clutched her gloves. "They were waiting... watching."

Cassian's jaw locked. "And running confirms it."

He placed a hand at the small of her back, guiding her through the gate as the guards rushed to attention.

"We increase security immediately," he ordered. "No one enters or leaves the grounds without my knowledge. Double the patrols at night. And send word to Gideon at first light."

"Yes, Your Grace," the guard replied.

Once they passed through the courtyard, Cassian paused, turning fully to Charlotte. Her blue eyes seemed furious.

"They mean to frighten us," she said. "To unsettle us."

"They will fail," he answered.

Her lips parted slightly, and Cassian realized, with startling clarity, that this woman had become everything to him. And Lord save those who meant to stand in their way.

"Come," he murmured. "We go inside. Tomorrow, we begin to hunt our enemy."

***

Sleep did not come easily.

Long after the manor had gone quiet, Charlotte lay in her bed staring into the darkness. She could still smell the scent of smoke, see the flames dancing behind her eyelids. And every time she drifted toward rest, she saw that shadowed figure by the gate, watching and waiting, and her chest tightened with dread.

At last, exhaustion won. But sleep brought no peace.

She could see fire. She could hear screams. She could smell the smoke pouring through the warehouse doors. Her hands were slipping on soaked floorboards. Edmund's mocking voice whispered that disaster followed her wherever she went. Then, she saw Cassian lying beneath fallen beams, motionless and cold.

"No, Cassian! Please..." she cried, thrashing against the nightmare.

She jolted awake with a gasp. Her nightdress was damp with cold sweat. Moonlight spilled in pale ribbons across the floor, but the quiet did nothing to steady her. Her breath trembled. She wrapped her arms around herself and froze as an unwelcome thought entered her mind: she did not want to be alone.

Charlotte slipped from the bed, drew her robe around her shoulders, and padded into the corridor. For a long moment, she stood before his door. She wondered if she should even be there. A proper duchess would turn back. A proper lady would compose herself. But propriety had never steadied her heartbeat, nor chased away shadows.

She knocked.

There was a pause, then the soft tread of bare feet. The door opened a fraction, revealing Cassian shirtless, with his hair tousled and his gaze sharp even in sleep.

"Charlotte?" The concern in his voice overtook the surprise. "What is it?"

She swallowed hard. "I..." Her composure wavered. "I dreamed you were hurt. I know it is foolish, but I cannot seem to catch my breath, and I..." She forced the words out. "I did not wish to be alone."

She didn't expect him to smile, and he didn't. But his face still changed enough for her to see understanding. They had both been through much that day.

He stepped back, opening the door wider. "Come in."

Inside, the room was warm from the embers in the hearth. Charlotte stood awkwardly for a moment, her hands twisting together.

Cassian watched her quietly. "You are safe, you know that," he said. "No one will harm you here."

She nodded, but her voice was barely a whisper when she asked. "May I... stay? Just for tonight?" Her cheeks warmed. "I only wish to sleep. Nothing more. I simply... Do not want to close my eyes alone."

Cassian didn't hesitate, though she saw his throat tighten, as if the request struck something deep within him.

"Yes, Charlotte." His tone was gentle. "You may stay."

He turned back the covers, and she slipped into the bed. When he lay beside her, she expected distance, a careful space between them. But when she shivered, he reached out slowly, as though giving her every chance to retreat, and drew her into his arms. Her cheek rested against his chest. His heartbeat was steady and strong beneath her ear.

"Breathe," he murmured.

She did. His warmth wrapped around her, and she felt something inside her unlock, some tight, fearful knot she had carried alone for too long.

"Thank you," she whispered after a while.

His hand brushed her back in a slow, calming stroke. "You need never fear seeking me," he said quietly. "Not in daylight, and not in darkness."

The room settled into stillness. Charlotte closed her eyes, her breath falling in rhythm with his. Fear ebbed. The nightmare receded. And in Cassian's arms, she finally slept.

Chapter Twenty-One

The night of the Cavendish Charity Ball arrived with a rustle of silk, whispered anticipation, and a flutter in Charlotte's chest she could not quite dispel. Miriam fastened the last pearl button at her back and stepped away so Charlotte might see herself in the looking glass.

Her gown, Lydia's masterpiece, was a dream of soft satin, fitted to her waist and flowing in gentle folds that shimmered when she moved. Tiny crystals, sewn by hand, traced the neckline like frost on morning glass. Charlotte scarcely recognized the woman staring back at her: poised and luminous, undeniably a duchess.

"His Grace will faint on the spot," Miriam said with a conspiratorial grin.

Charlotte laughed, though nerves chased the sound. "Let us hope he remains upright. I should hate to explain such a scene to the ton."

When she descended the staircase, she found Cassian waiting below.

He turned at the sound of her approach and stopped. For one suspended moment, he simply stared. He wore no guarded expression, just... astonishment.

Heat rushed to Charlotte's cheeks. "Do I pass inspection, Your Grace?"

Cassian closed the remaining distance between them, his gaze moving over her slowly and with reverence, as though afraid to break whatever spell lingered in the air.

"You are..." He paused, searching for the correct word. "Radiant."

Her breath caught. "Thank you," she managed.

He offered his arm, and she placed her gloved hand atop his sleeve. That single point of contact sent a ripple through her body, steadying and thrilling all at once.

When they arrived at the Cavendish townhouse, it glowed like a jewel, welcoming them. Gas lamps lined the steps, and inside, chandeliers dripped golden light over polished floors. Musicians played a lively quadrille, while gowns swirled, jewels flashed, and laughter rose beneath the glittering cascade of crystal.

Charlotte had attended such events before, long ago. Then, she remembered longing for attention, for admiration and for affection.

Tonight, her attention strayed only to the man at her side.

Cassian guided her through the throng with calm authority, acknowledging acquaintances with a nod, and ignoring gossiping matrons entirely. More than one pair of eyes followed them, some curious, others covetous. Charlotte should have felt exposed.

Instead, she felt seen.

"I had forgotten how dazzling these affairs can be," she said as they paused near the dance area.

"Dazzling," he agreed. "Though I suspect that impression has more to do with you than with chandeliers."

She turned to him, startled into a soft laugh. "Cassian, if you continue in this manner, you will have all of London believing you a charming man."

He leaned closer, lowering his voice so only she could hear. "Let London believe what it wishes. I am speaking only to you."

Her pulse fluttered. It was ridiculous, for she was no silly debutante, yet his words washed over her with disarming sweetness.

A waltz began. Cassian extended his hand.

"May I?"

"Yes," she breathed.

From the first moment he swayed her to the music, she had to admit that she had not expected him to be such a dancer. Cassian moved with quiet certainty, guiding her through each turn of the waltz as though he had been made for it. She had heard whispers over the years that the Duke of Duskbourne never danced, not since the tragedy that befell him. And Gideon himself had joked, only an hour earlier, that the evening might freeze over if Cassian so much as put his lady on a dance floor.

And yet, here they were, in perfect rhythm.

A murmur rippled through the ballroom as they passed, and the crowd parted for them in graceful waves. Those not dancing paused to watch, while whispers trailed behind them like golden ribbons.

"Is that the Duke?"

"I have never seen him waltz..."

"Look how they suit each other... good heavens!"

Charlotte should have flushed with self-consciousness. Instead, fire bloomed in her chest. She felt more alive than ever before, as Cassian's eyes remained on hers, never wandering, never flickering toward their audience. The ballroom blurred at the edges, and it felt like they were dancing alone.

"You are staring," he murmured. Impossibly, he smiled.

"You are dancing," she countered. "I have been assured that never happens."

"Gideon talks too much," Cassian replied dryly.

Charlotte laughed, but the sound died quickly as he drew her closer. Not indecently so, but it was enough for his breath to brush her temple, and also enough for her pulse to trip into chaos.

"You waltz beautifully," she whispered.

He lowered his head, drinking in the sight of her. "I waltz beautifully with *you*. That is the distinction."

Heat swept through her, swift and consuming. Around them, gowns swirled and boots glided, but Charlotte felt the world shrinking to the precise space where their bodies met and moved. They magically found themselves in an intimate orbit of two, bound by music and something far more intoxicating.

"You astonish me, Charlotte," he said in a tone that trembled through her. "Every hour I spend in your company, I find myself wanting... more."

Her breath caught. "More?"

His thumb brushed lightly against her back, in a gentle, possessive stroke that made her knees weaken mid-step.

"When we return home," Cassian whispered, and his eyes darkened at his own words, "I will show you precisely what I mean."

Her heart stuttered. The promise hung between them, potent and unspoken in its full meaning. She felt the truth of it in his touch, in the way his gaze lingered on her lips, and in the way her body leaned instinctively closer.

"What are you doing to me?" she managed to say, as she felt her body melting in his arms.

It was as if both were utterly unhinged, allowing themselves things that were never allowed before. And they were both relishing the moment.

Just as he leaned in dangerously close, making her entire body shiver with delight, the music stopped. However, he did not immediately release her hand. Instead, he lifted it slowly, his gaze never leaving hers, and pressed a deliberate, lingering kiss to her knuckles. The gesture was chaste enough for any ballroom observer, yet the heat that shot through her arm was anything but proper.

A soft sigh rippled through nearby ladies. Several fans fluttered at once.

Cassian offered his arm, and Charlotte found her voice only long enough to whisper, "You will cause a scandal if you continue in this fashion."

"Then it will be the first scandal I have ever welcomed," he murmured back.

He led her from the dance area, and together they approached the refreshments table where Lydia, Nicholas, and Gideon stood in lively conversation. Gideon spotted them first, grinning.

"Well, well," he drawled. "And here I feared the duke had forgotten which end of the ballroom was which. Clearly, marriage has worked miracles."

Charlotte tried to compose herself, but Lydia's eyes sparkled far too knowingly.

"My dear," Lydia said, leaning close, "your cheeks are positively aflame. Either the ballroom is far too warm, or your husband dances exceedingly well."

Charlotte swatted her arm, though laughter burst from her despite her best efforts. Even Nicholas, normally so guarded where his sister was concerned, shook his head with amused resignation.

"I should have expected no less," Nicholas said, directing a pointed glance at Cassian. "My wife designs gowns that turn heads. My sister manages to collect gossip like silk collects light. Between the two of them, how can a mere duke hope to go unnoticed?"

"By standing very still and speaking rarely," Cassian replied dryly.

Gideon barked a laugh. "Ah, so that is your strategy. And here I thought you were simply surly by nature."

Lydia covered her smile behind her fan. Charlotte nearly choked on her lemonade. Soon enough, the group fell into an easy rhythm of stories, teasing, and gentle barbs tossed about like a well-practiced reel.

"I will never forgive you for that waltz, Charlotte," Gideon declared dramatically, placing a hand to his heart. "You have ruined my evening. Every dance partner will now seem a tragic disappointment."

Charlotte laughed. "You will survive, my lord. I have seen you charm half the women in London before supper."

"And the other half after," Lydia added brightly.

Gideon gasped. "Duchess, you wound me."

Nicholas snorted into his glass. "If your ego is dented by simple truth, Harrow, it is more fragile than I supposed."

"My ego," Gideon countered, "is indestructible. I merely enjoy being admired, preferably aloud and often."

Charlotte pressed a gloved hand to her lips to stifle giggles. Cassian leaned in slightly, not enough to draw notice, but enough that she could hear the rumble of quiet amusement in his voice.

"You find us entertaining," he murmured.

"I find you *all* insufferable," she whispered back. "But in a most pleasant way."

Lydia looped her arm through Charlotte's. "Tell me, dearest, did you see how every lady stopped to gape when the duke led you onto the floor? I thought three women would swoon outright."

"They did," Gideon said. "One nearly collapsed onto the refreshment table. I considered catching her, but alas, I was holding a very good brandy at the time."

Charlotte burst into laughter, unable to help herself. The sound came so freely that she barely recognized it as her own.

She felt *alive.*

She felt *seen.*

And most of all, she felt *happy.*

It was a rare and fragile thing, happiness. She had not realized how dearly she missed it until it settled over her like a soft shawl. Tonight, surrounded by elegance and companionship and the quiet strength of the man at her side, Charlotte allowed herself to savour every breath of it.

When Cassian offered his arm once more, she took it without hesitation. Whatever awaited tomorrow, whatever danger, secrets, or enemies in the dark, tonight remained untouched.

Tonight, she felt cherished.

And she was grateful for every exquisite, intoxicating moment.

Chapter Twenty-Two

For a while, the ball unfolded with enviable perfection.

Charlotte's laughter warmed the space between them, and Cassian found himself, against all reason, relaxed. He couldn't take his eyes off of Charlotte, exactly because he knew that every eye in the room followed her.

At first, he thought it was because she glowed with such effortless grace that it made every man jealous of him. The thought made him more proud than he was willing to admit. In fact, by all accounts, it was shaping up to be a perfect evening.

But then, Cassian felt the shift. He *noticed* it in the murmurs, in the ripple, and in the sudden prickle at the back of his neck.

He caught, from the corner of his eye, two matrons whispering behind their fans. A young lord snickered as a slip of folded paper was passed to him, which he opened, read, and promptly shared with a cluster of debutantes who gasped in delight and horror.

Cassian swallowed heavily. That wasn't a good sign. In fact, it was a very bad sign, a sign that something was terribly wrong.

Cassian crossed to Nicholas, who was lingering near the refreshments with a few other gentlemen.

"Nicholas," Cassian said quietly, eyeing the piece of paper and what hand it was in at the moment, "what are they passing?"

Charlotte's brother followed Cassian's line of sight, and momentarily, his expression grew dark. When the next lord, some idle young baron, received one of the mysterious slips, Nicholas strode forward and plucked it straight from the man's hand.

The baron jolted back. "I beg your pardon, Your Grace, but that is private—"

Nicholas didn't say anything. He merely skimmed through what was on it, and Cassian watched as his expression blossomed from confusion to shock and finally to fury.

"What is it?" Cassian demanded.

Nicholas hesitated, then handed him the slip. Cassian unfolded it. He needed only one line to understand. His blood turned to ice.

My dearest Edmund, my heart is yours... always.

Charlotte M.

It was Charlotte's letter, but not the original. Someone had gone through the painstaking effort of printing it out and then distributing it... *weaponizing* it.

Her private letters had been copied for sport, for scandal, for humiliation.

Cassian refolded the paper once. It crumpled in his fist.

He looked up. "Who has done this?"

Nicholas stepped closer, glancing around. "Good God... they're everywhere."

Indeed, they were. More scraps were passed from hand to hand, hidden behind gloves and fans. Young ladies were whispering. Gentlemen were smirking. A cluster of dowagers was pretending to be shocked while revelling in every syllable.

Cassian's fingers crushed the paper in his fist.

Nicholas swore under his breath. "It must be Larke. He means to ruin her."

Ruin her.

The very idea sent a bolt of rage through Cassian so sharp he almost saw red. He glanced across the ballroom and saw *her...* Charlotte, who had been deceived, wounded, and used, the same Charlotte who had finally begun to smile again, on this night, of all nights.

Cassian forced himself to breathe. The fury was too large to contain, but he would not erupt here, not in the midst of the vultures.

"I will not allow this to stand," he snarled silently.

Nicholas nodded sharply. "What do you plan to do?"

"First," Cassian replied, eyes already tracking Charlotte across the room, "I remove my wife from this cesspool of gossip. Then I find the man responsible. And when I do..."

His hand curled at his side.

"I will destroy him."

Across the ballroom, Charlotte laughed at something Lydia had said. She was still blissfully unaware of the storm gathering at her back. She looked radiant, hopeful, open in a way Cassian had not seen since their wedding. The sight made the betrayal all the more unforgivable.

He drew a breath, calming his expression and schooling his features into composed neutrality. Slowly, he approached

Charlotte with careful control, masking every trace of fury. She turned toward him, smiling. She was still glowing from the dance, still unaware of the poison spreading through the ballroom like spilled ink.

"Cassian," she said softly, "is everything all right?"

He offered his arm. "Come with me," he murmured. "We are leaving."

Her brows knit. "Leaving? Already? But—"

"I will explain," he said gently, but firmly. "Not here."

Charlotte hesitated only a moment before nodding. She trusted him. He saw it in her eyes, and the knowledge cut him as deeply as it steadied him. He guided her through the ballroom as Gideon cleared a subtle path. Nicholas and Lydia followed at a distance, watchful but silent. Not a single whisper reached Charlotte's ears. Cassian made certain of it, intercepting glances with a stare that froze tongues mid-syllable.

They exited under the glitter of the chandeliers, and only when the great doors shut behind them did Charlotte release a quiet breath.

"Cassian," she tried again, more confused this time, "what has happened?"

"In the carriage," he said.

The ride began in silence. Only once the driver's whip cracked and the wheels began to turn did Cassian reach into his coat. He withdrew the crumpled sheet, which was the single copy he had kept.

He looked at her, knowing he had to choose his words very carefully. "What I am about to show you... is cruel. And it is not a reflection of you. Do you understand?"

She blinked. The worry in her eyes sharpened into fear. "Cassian, please... what is it?"

He placed the paper into her trembling hands.

One glance... that was all it took.

Her breath hitched, and her gloved fingers crushed the page as though it had burned her. Colour drained from her face. She looked at him, wide-eyed and horrified.

"This was private," she whispered. "Those were *mine*. How... how could—"

Her voice snapped under the weight of humiliation. And then she broke. Tears spilled in helpless, shaking waves, and she pressed her hands over her face as though she could hide from the world and from him, from the shame being paraded in print.

He moved to her at once.

"Charlotte," he murmured, gathering her in his arms without hesitation.

She collapsed against his chest, sobs shaking her slender frame. He held her with one hand, cradling the back of her head, and the other drawing her tightly against him, creating a shield where no eyes could reach her.

"I was so foolish," she choked out. "So naïve. They will laugh... everyone will laugh—"

"No," he promised her. "They will not. I will not allow it."

Charlotte did not stop crying. The minutes slipped by, marked only by the rocking of the carriage and the soft, broken sounds she tried to suppress. Cassian held her through all of it, without a word, without rushing her grief or offering hollow comforts. He simply *remained.*

Her tears soaked into his coat. Her fingers clutched him as though he were the last solid thing in a world turned treacherous. And Cassian, who once believed he had nothing left to give a woman, found he had patience for her sorrow.

When fresh sobs overtook her, he only drew her closer.

When shame shook her shoulders, he smoothed her hair and whispered, "You are not alone."

When she tried to apologize through gasping breaths, he silenced her softly. "There is nothing to apologize for."

Eventually, the sobs dulled, leaving only quiet tremors in her frame. She stayed wrapped in his arms until the carriage slowed and the familiar outline of Duskbourne came into view.

Cassian did not release her immediately, not until the wheels ground to a halt and the footman stepped forward with a lantern.

"We are home," he murmured, brushing a tear from her cheek.

She nodded at him, with eyes that were swollen and red, and when she spoke, her voice was little more than a whisper. "Thank you... for everything."

He helped her down from the carriage, shielding her from the curious glance of the footman, and escorted her inside. The manor was still, as the hour was late. The candlelight was soft enough to hide the worst of her distress. At the staircase, Charlotte paused.

"I should retire," she said, trembling again. "I—I do not want to be seen. I cannot bear it."

Cassian bowed his head slightly. "Of course."

She managed a small, grateful smile and slipped upstairs. He watched until she disappeared behind her chamber door. He *should* have left it at that. He should have allowed her space and solitude.

But as he turned to leave, something inside him twisted. It was the painful and unwelcome memory of the nights he had drowned in grief alone, nights that could sometimes feel like a blade.

He hesitated. Then turned back.

Three steps brought him to her door again. His hand hovered over the panel before he knocked gently. A faint sound came from within. The door opened a few inches.

Charlotte stood there, still in her gown, with her hair loosened from its pins and her eyes heavy with exhaustion and sorrow.

"Cassian?" she whispered.

He met her gaze. "Forgive me. I could not leave you like this."

For a moment, she said nothing. Then she stepped aside in an echo of a silent invitation, and he entered, the door closing softly behind them.

***

She turned away from him the moment he entered. If she faced him, she feared she would break all over again.

Her voice emerged in a whisper. "My reputation is ruined."

Cassian said nothing at first. She heard only his quiet breath behind her. She pressed on, with words spilling faster, sharp with despair.

"And now yours is, too. They will mock *you* for my foolishness. I have brought you shame, and I cannot—"

"Stop." His voice cut through her panic with sudden force.

That was when she turned. Cassian crossed the space between them in three decisive strides. There was fire in his eyes, cold and controlled, but burning all the same.

"Do not take the blame for the sins of a liar," he said. "You wrote in innocence, in hope. There is no shame in that." His jaw tightened. "The shame belongs to the man who betrayed you. And I will find him."

"They will laugh at me," she whispered. "At us."

Cassian shook his head, eyes never leaving hers. "Let them laugh. Let them choke on their gossip and their bile. Their voices mean nothing. *You* have done nothing wrong."

He could see how vulnerable she felt, and a tidal wave of tenderness washed over him. |I feel so exposed," she whispered, "so foolish, so... ugly."

"No," he said softly. He reached up, brushing the back of his fingers gently along her cheek. "You are *not* ugly, Charlotte. You are the most breathtaking woman I have ever seen. You have strength, and grace, and a heart capable of feeling more deeply than most dare dream."

Her breath trembled. "You cannot mean that."

"I do... Tonight, you walked into that ballroom, and the world noticed. I noticed. And I have not looked away since."

Cassian stepped closer still, his hand moving to the nape of her neck, cradling it with protective tenderness.

"Whoever tries to destroy you must answer to me," he murmured. "You are not alone, Charlotte."

The final wall he had held between them gave way.

"Cassian..." she breathed.

Slowly, giving her every chance to pull away, he lowered his forehead to hers. She closed her eyes, and he felt the warmth of her breath brush his lips. His thumb stroked her cheek, and she leaned into his touch.

Then, he kissed her. Charlotte's fingers curled into his shirt, pulling him closer, and Cassian's hand slid to her waist, holding her as though he feared she might shatter.

His fingers weaved into her hair as he angled her closer. The tenderness didn't disappear, but it transformed and grew. His lips tasted her, savoured her, as though he had been starving for a long time.

Charlotte trembled, and he felt her melt into him. Cassian's arm wrapped around her waist, steady and sure, pulling her flush against him as the kiss grew more intoxicating, turning into slow fire, spreading through blood and breath and bone.

Gently, he moved them back toward her bed, relinquishing her of the rest of her hair pins. He pulled the tied ribbons that held her gown in place, and the gown slid down her naked body.

Her skin prickled with goosepimples as the cold air met it, but he pressed himself against her to warm her back up. Her hands stayed locked around his neck, keeping him close, refusing distance, even as he lay her down upon the bed and shifted between her legs.

He couldn't remember unbuttoning his trousers, only the taste of her lips, the soft gasps that escaped her mouth, and the way her body arched toward him like it had been waiting for this moment all along.

"Oh..." she moaned loudly as he pressed his manhood against her wet heat.

The sound went straight to his core, nearly undoing him. He pulled away only for a moment, wanting to drink in the sight of her. He had never seen her more beautiful than she was now: her eyes dark with yearning, her lips parted, and her entire body trembling with need.

Cassian let his fingers trail down her stomach, over soft, heated skin, until he reached her centre. She was already wet, aching for him. He wanted to taste her again, to lose himself between his thighs, but he couldn't pull away from her mouth. Instead, he slipped a finger inside of her, groaning softly at the way she clenched around him.

"You are so wet for me..." he murmured against her lips and felt her shiver at the words.

When he added another finger, she gasped. Pleasure and pain tangled in that sound, the sweetest thing he'd ever heard. Her nails dug into his shoulders, sharp enough to sting, but he welcomed it. He bit her lower lip, then soothed it with his tongue, unable to stop himself from pressing closer.

When he finally positioned himself at her entrance, he paused. Their foreheads touched, and their breaths mingled. Her eyes found his.

"I'll be gentle," he promised softly.

She nodded, and he pushed inside, slowly and reverently. The tight, silken heat of her made his breath catch. He could feel her body yield, stretch, welcome him. Every instinct in him screamed to move, to take, but he forced himself to go slow, to memorize every inch, every sound she made as he filled her completely.

Her legs wrapped around his hips, pulling him deeper. The rhythm they found was raw and consuming, their bodies moving harder, faster, until he couldn't tell where he ended and she began. Her hands clutched at him like she was afraid he'd vanish, and when she tightened around him, he knew she was close.

Cassian drove into her once more, again and again, grinding against her, kissing her like he was starving. When she came, it was with a cry that undid him completely. Her body convulsed around him, and the sensation tore through his control. He followed her over that edge, shuddering, thrusting once more before stilling inside of her.

For a moment that seemed eternal, there was only breath. He pulled her into his arms, with the wild rhythm of her heartbeat against his own.

"I love you, Cassian..." he heard her say sleepily.

The words felt like a blow, too soft to defend himself against. He wanted to say it back, but it caught somewhere in his throat. Instead, he just held her tighter, pressing a kiss to her hair as her breathing evened out, and let the silence swallow the things he could not yet say.

Chapter Twenty-Three

Cassian woke before dawn, as he always did, though this morning the waking felt different. For a moment, he simply lay still, with awareness slowly settling over him. Charlotte was still blissfully asleep by his side.

Cassian closed his eyes briefly. He had held her until sleep finally claimed her, but he had not said the words she clearly needed. She stirred faintly beside him, and he knew if he stayed another moment, he would lose the will to leave at all.

He slipped from the bed with careful movements, drawing the blankets over her shoulders. Charlotte did not wake. He cast one more glance before he reached for the door handle, then let himself out.

Nicholas waited for him on the manor steps, just as they had agreed the previous night.

"You're certain you wish to go through with our plan today?" Nicholas asked.

Cassian adjusted his coat. "I will not waste a single hour. Edmund Larke did not vanish into thin air. Men who hide leave trails, and I intend to follow every one."

Nicholas gave a curt nod. "Then let us begin."

They kept their investigation quiet. Discretion mattered, as Charlotte's name was not to be dragged further through public mud.

Their first destination was an inn at the edge of town, a place known for travellers and gossip both. The innkeeper was eager to help when Cassian laid a heavy coin on the counter, and he admitted he had seen Edmund weeks ago, looking nervous, hurried, and ducking from windows as though fearing discovery. He had spoken to no one for long, but he had accepted a letter that seemed to alarm him.

"From whom?" Cassian pressed.

The man only shrugged. "No name. But he paid his bill before dawn and left in a panic."

At the next stop, a small nearby market, Nicholas coaxed a merchant into talking. The merchant remembered Edmund's face. He remembered, too, that he had exchanged some valuables for unmarked coin.

"He was planning to run," Nicholas murmured as they stepped away.

"Or waiting for something, and when it arrived, he fled," Cassian replied.

Their final inquiry of the morning led them to a dockhand at a smaller inn near the post road. This man, Mr. Harland, had already proven to have a loose tongue and a fondness for coin.

Cassian set another shilling on the table. "You were saying..."

Harland glanced at the door, then leaned in. "I remember the fellow ye described. Edmund Larke. Nervous sort. Always watchin' over his shoulder. He came through here about a fortnight past. Didn't stay long. Didn't want to be seen."

"Did he speak to anyone?" Cassian asked.

Harland nodded slowly. "Aye. He waited until near closing. Then a gentleman came. Well-dressed, though tryin' to hide it. They spoke soft, but I heard enough. They were speakin' of travel. Of waitin' until the chaos in London settled." He lowered his voice. "The name Keaton was mentioned twice. Said the Keatons owed him favours."

Nicholas met Cassian's gaze. The tavern keeper's earlier rumour had just found its teeth.

"Where were they headed?" Nicholas asked.

Harland lifted one shoulder. "Couldn't say. But the Keatons have a house east of here. Not far from the cliffs near Saltbourne. Folk know them. Old money. Fine reputation. The kind who host poets and pretend they discovered 'em." He snorted. "Wouldn't surprise me if they sheltered a coward, too."

Coward.

The word suited Edmund far too well.

Cassian reached into his coat and placed another coin on the table, not out of generosity, but to buy silence as well as information.

"You will speak of this to no one," he said.

Harland nodded vigorously, snatching the coin.

Cassian rose, and so did Nicholas. They left the inn in a hurry and headed for the Keaton estate, which sat perched upon the cliffs. Seagulls wheeled overhead, and the distant crash of waves struck the rocks below. It was an idyllic scene that belied the ugliness of the truth Cassian sought.

Cassian and Nicholas were shown into a small receiving parlour, and the footman hurried off to fetch the master of the house. Cassian stood with his hands clasped behind his back, outwardly calm, though impatience burned beneath his skin.

It did not take long for Mr. and Mrs. Keaton to appear. Mr. Keaton, who was a tall, silver-haired gentleman with a scholar's posture, offered a stiff bow. His wife, a pale woman with cool eyes and a forced smile, inclined her head.

"I do not believe we have had the pleasure," Mr. Keaton began. "I am Arthur Keaton, and this is my wife, Elise."

Cassian returned the bow. "Cassian Oberon, Duke of Duskbourne. This is Nicholas Montclair, Duke of Hawthorne."

At the names, both Keatons stiffened, caught between surprise and sudden caution.

"Your Graces," Mrs. Keaton said, dipping into a hurried curtsy. "We are honoured, of course, but we must confess ourselves bewildered. To what honour do we owe such... distinguished callers?"

Cassian did not waste a moment.

"We come on a matter of urgency," he said. "We seek information about a man who, we have reason to believe, passed through here and may have approached you for help. His name is Edmund Larke."

At once, Mr. Keaton's expression shuttered. Mrs. Keaton's hand tightened on her shawl.

Nicholas noticed it too. "You recognize the name."

Mr. Keaton cleared his throat. "We... have acquaintances in literary circles. We have heard it before. But what business does this Edmund have with you?"

Cassian stepped forward. "That is not your concern. What matters now is that he has committed harm against my duchess, and I mean to find him. We have reason to believe he sought shelter with you."

"Your Grace," Mrs. Keaton protested, "surely you must be mistaken. We offer lodging to artists and patrons of the arts, yes, but we do not harbour criminals."

Cassian studied her. She avoided his gaze. Her husband suddenly found the carpet very interesting.

Cassian reached into his coat and withdrew a pouch of coins, placing it on a small side table with quiet deliberation.

"You will forgive me," Cassian pointed out, "if I do not rely on polite assurances alone. We are not here to accuse you, only to learn what you know of a man who has taken my wife's peace."

Silence taunted them.

Then, Mr. Keaton's shoulders slumped. "He did come to us," Keaton confessed at last. "Briefly, though. He arrived near midnight some weeks ago, demanding refuge. He said he needed to disappear, and that if we turned him away, we would regret it."

Mrs. Keaton had a brittle dignity that was now cracking at the edges. "He was... not the man we once knew. We sheltered him two nights, no more. He frightened the servants. And *us*."

Cassian's voice sharpened. "Where did he go when he left?"

"We truly do not know," Keaton insisted. "He would not give details, only that he needed distance and time."

Cassian inclined his head once. "If he returns—"

Mrs. Keaton cut in quickly, "We will send word to Duskbourne at once. We want no further part in this."

Cassian retrieved the coin pouch, leaving only a modest amount behind.

"Then we are finished here," he said. "Pray he does not darken your door again."

The Keatons exhaled in shaky relief as Cassian and Nicholas took their leave.

"Well, I suppose that is all for today," Nicholas announced, sounding even more disappointed than Cassian.

"Yes," Cassian agreed. "But this is not over."

They agreed to regroup once Cassian sent word of their next move, but as Cassian rode alone toward Duskbourne, irritation and frustration rode with him. Edmund had slipped through their grasp. The Keatons' crumbs of information were enough to confirm the danger, yet not enough to seize it.

For a man accustomed to control, Cassian found failure a bitter, unfamiliar taste.

By the time the estate came into view, shadows had swallowed the sky, and a storm threatened on the horizon. He dismounted with stiff movements, tossed the reins to a waiting groom, and strode into the manor with the tight, coiled energy of a man who could neither fight nor rest.

Charlotte met him in the hall.

Her expression softened at the sight of him. "Cassian... you're home."

She stepped forward, resting her hands lightly on his arms. She leaned in to kiss him, but he stepped back. Surprise flickered across her face, followed by a hurt she tried to mask.

"I... thought perhaps you would join me for supper," she said gently. "I had Cook prepare a few of—"

"I am not hungry," he interrupted. His voice came out colder than he intended, but he did not correct it.

Charlotte blinked, steadying herself. "I understand. Then perhaps later, when you—"

"I have matters to attend to," he said. "It has been a long day. I wish to retire."

A faint breath escaped her, something like disappointment, or worse, resignation. "Of course," she murmured. "Good night, Cassian."

He inclined his head and turned away far too quickly, walking toward his chamber with a stride that felt like escape rather than dismissal. Minutes later, he was sitting alone in the dim glow of the fire, with his elbows on his knees and his hands clasped tightly. The room felt suffocating, though no one else was in it.

He exhaled.

Why had he spoken to her that way? She had greeted him with warmth and affection, and he had given her nothing in return... less than nothing. He had slapped away the tenderness she offered so freely.

He reminded himself that tenderness was dangerous. Desire was dangerous, too. But love... love was *fatal.*

He had learned that truth with Eleanor. He had buried that truth in the ground with her. And now Charlotte was stirring feelings he had sworn never to touch again.

Desire pulled him toward her. Fear yanked him back. And guilt sat between them like a ghost.

If I love her, I will lose her. If I let her in, I will destroy her.

Charlotte deserved safety, laughter, light, not a man haunted by ashes and graves. She didn't deserve a husband who feared a future more than he feared any enemy.

And yet... everything that happened between them was branded inside his mind for all eternity. He cared for her, and that terrified him more than losing any fortune, title, or friend.

Sleep did not come. He did not even try.

For how could he sleep when he was wrestling with a heart that refused to obey him?

Chapter Twenty-Four

Breakfast at Duskbourne had never felt so quiet.

The silverware gleamed, the tea steamed, and Cook had prepared an array of dishes that should have filled the room with warmth, but instead, the morning air hung cold and heavy, like frost settling over glass.

Charlotte sat at her place, staring at the untouched slice of toast on her plate. Across the long table, Cassian was reading the morning paper as though it demanded his full concentration. He had greeted her politely when he entered. It was not polite enough to be cruel, but distant enough to remind her that their previous closeness had slipped through her fingers like sand.

She lifted her teacup, forcing composure into every movement, and decided to ask the first thing that came to mind.

"Did you sleep well, Your Grace?"

Cassian did not look up. "Well enough," he replied, turning a page.

She glanced toward him. "I was awake for quite some time. I did not hear you come to bed."

"That is because I did not," he said without inflection. "There was work to be done."

Charlotte swallowed, nodding as though the answer had not pierced her. "I see."

Another pause followed, longer and colder.

She tried again. "Will you be in your study today?"

"For part of the morning."

"And later?"

His eyes flicked up at last. "What matters require my schedule, Duchess?"

She stiffened. *Duchess.* Not *Charlotte.*

"None," she answered quietly. "I merely asked."

He offered a curt nod. "Then I shall be occupied. There is much to address."

Her chest tightened. She set down her teacup with care lest it betray the tremor starting in her fingers.

"Of course," she murmured.

They lapsed back into silence. The only sounds were the faint clink of porcelain and the slow, deliberate turning of Cassian's newspaper. Charlotte's appetite evaporated. She pushed her plate gently away and folded her napkin in her lap, each precise crease giving her a sense of small control.

Last night's rejection still stung. He had held her as though she mattered, kissed her as though she were precious, and then shut her out once the passion had cooled. She felt foolish for having let herself hope.

Cassian finally set the paper aside. He looked at her then, but whatever emotion flickered in his eyes vanished before she could read it.

"Shall I have the carriage brought round for you later?" he asked. "If you intend to go into town."

"No, thank you," she informed him, dabbing the corner of her mouth with her napkin, despite the fact that she had not eaten a single bite. "Since I have plans of my own, I shall bid you good morning."

Charlotte turned and left the breakfast room. She paused in the corridor, drawing a steadying breath. Then she lifted her chin and walked on. She found Miriam nearby, polishing the silver trays with practiced focus.

"Miriam," Charlotte said, summoning composure, "please have my cloak and bonnet brought to the foyer. I intend to go into town."

Miriam hesitated. "At once, Your Grace. Shall I accompany you?"

"Yes," Charlotte answered. "I will not remain indoors today."

Only once she was cloaked and gloved did she step outside. She expected the walk to clear her head. Instead, each step felt heavier than the one before.

If Cassian would not speak to her, then fine. She would occupy herself. She would *stand*, not fold.

The outskirts of the town came into view soon enough. Houses lined the streets and smoke curled from the chimneys. At first, nothing seemed amiss. A shopkeeper who was sweeping his stoop paused to bow politely. Two young ladies, arm in arm, dipped their heads in greeting.

Then she heard it.

"...so desperate, can you imagine?"

"...love letters, and to a common poet of all things..."

"...Duskbourne's duchess—what a scandal..."

Her steps faltered. Miriam stiffened behind her. Charlotte lifted her chin and continued, ignoring the sudden hush that followed her passing. But the whispers picked back up as soon as her back was turned.

"They say she practically chased the duke, trying to save her reputation..."

"...those letters were pathetic—begging, pleading..."

"...ruined before her own wedding day..."

Charlotte's spine went rigid. A group of older women clustered near the milliner's door stopped talking altogether, staring at her with barely concealed fascination. When Charlotte met their eyes, one of them gave an insipid, pitying smile that felt like a slap.

Her pride wavered. Heat prickled behind her eyes.

She turned sharply into the nearest shop, which was a modest mercer's, to escape the accusing eyes and poisonous murmurs. Once inside, she gripped the edge of a display table to steady herself.

Miriam stepped close. "Your Grace... we may return home. You do not need to endure this."

Charlotte drew a slow breath, pressing back the tremor in her chest.

"If I flee," she whispered, "then they win. They will say I am hiding. I refuse to cower because others choose cruelty."

Miriam bowed her head. "Then I am with you. Always."

Charlotte managed a strained smile of gratitude. But the truth burned beneath her skin. She had thought she was strong enough. It was all a lie.

Her voice shook despite her resolve. "Let us finish what we came for, Miriam. Then we will return."

Miriam nodded. Charlotte forced her breathing to steady and stepped back outside. The whispers resumed, and each one cut a little deeper. By the time she reached the end of the lane, she realized she had not escaped anything.

She had only confronted it and found herself bleeding from wounds she could not hide.

***

Charlotte returned to Duskbourne with her pride scraped thin and her heart heavy from the day's cruelty. The manor, usually a comfort, felt colder than the streets she had just escaped. She handed her bonnet and gloves to Miriam and made her way down the corridor, intent on retreating to her chambers.

But as she drew near Cassian's study, she slowed, hearing voices.

Nicholas.

Her brother's deep tone was unmistakable and urgent. She paused, listening despite herself.

"...she will not like it," Nicholas murmured.

"She is not to be involved. I will not risk it," Cassian snapped in reply. "That is final."

Charlotte's pulse quickened. Before she could think better of it, she pushed open the door. Cassian and Nicholas both turned sharply. Their expressions of guilt and tension tangled together, telling her more than any words could.

"Good afternoon," she told them, sounding amused. "Nicholas. Cassian. I didn't realize you were meeting."

Nicholas recovered first, offering a fleeting smile. "Charlotte, we were just—"

"Speaking in whispers about me?" she cut in. "Yes, I gathered."

Cassian stepped forward. "This is not a matter you need to concern yourself with—"

"No," she snapped, surprising even herself with the ice in her tone. "You do not get to push me aside again."

The room went still.

Nicholas cleared his throat. "Charlotte, it is not my place to—"

She turned on him sharply. "If it concerns me, it *is* your place. And my right to know. Do not tell me otherwise."

Nicholas hesitated, then looked to Cassian, silently asking for permission.

Cassian's jaw flexed. "No."

"Cassian!" Her voice rose. "I am not a child. I am not porcelain. And I will not be sheltered while my name is torn apart."

He closed his eyes briefly, as though fighting himself. Charlotte pressed on.

"What plan were you forming?"

Nicholas inhaled deeply. "We wanted to send Edmund a letter to draw him out, to make it seem like it's from you. But the trouble is, we do not know where to send it. If he is moving about, it may never reach him."

Charlotte drew in a steadying breath. The memory came clear as though it had been marked on the edge of a page.

"When he spoke of traveling," she said, "he told me there was a place in town where a friend of his would fetch any letters I left. A small, unremarked post, behind the apothecary, by the lane that leads to the market. I once left a note there when he said he would be away, and someone took it in the night. If he has acquaintances who shelter him, that is where one of them might look."

Cassian cut in sharply. "It is reckless. We don't know who picks them up. We don't know where Edmund is. It could expose her to danger."

Charlotte met his gaze head-on. "I am already exposed."

He flinched.

She stepped closer. "Cassian, I walked through town today. They whispered. They stared. They tore me apart with nothing but their tongues. Hiding will not save me. Doing nothing will not save me."

"And offering yourself as bait?" he returned. "That will?"

"It gives us a chance to force him out of his hiding," she insisted. "A chance to end this and to regain control. And I will not cower when I can fight."

For a moment, she thought she could see fear in his eyes. "You could be hurt."

"I already am," she replied softly. "But if we do this, at least the pain means something."

Cassian raked a hand through his hair and turned away, staring at the fire. "I will not send you out alone."

"You won't," she said. "My maid will walk with me, as always. I will leave the letter at the drop point. Nothing more."

Cassian faced her again, conflict etched in every line of him. She held his gaze without wavering.

At last, he exhaled. "If we do this...we do it *my* way, with precautions and with eyes on every corner. If I sense danger, we end it immediately. Is that understood?"

Charlotte nodded once. "Understood."

Nicholas inclined his head. "Then it seems we have a plan."

About fifteen minutes later, he excused himself and left them alone. Cassian remained by the desk, hands braced on its edge as though he needed the wood to anchor him.

"Charlotte, we need to discuss this in detail first."

She met his gaze, bracing herself for distance again. She could not bear another morning like the last, another moment of him pushing her away under the guise of protection. Before he could speak another word, Charlotte moved.

She stepped into his space, rose on her toes, and kissed him.

It was not a timid kiss. This one was bold and certain; a decision rather than a question. Her hands slid to the lapels of his coat, holding him there, as though daring him to retreat again.

Cassian froze for a heartbeat. Then he answered. His hands found her waist, pulling her closer, and the kiss deepened with sudden heat. All the restraint he carried seemed to fracture at once. She could feel his hunger, just like she felt her own taking over.

Charlotte felt her breath leave her, felt the world tilt as his mouth moved against hers with urgency and longing that stole every thought she had. She led him back, toward the chaise lounge in the corner of his study, by the bookshelf.

Pulling away from their kiss, she pushed him down. He looked utterly bewildered, as if he had no idea what was going on. In a way, she didn't, either. So, she let her instinct guide her as she spread her legs and sat on his lap, her skirts pooled around her.

She grabbed his face and continued kissing him, moving her tongue deep inside, claiming him as her own, just like he had claimed her the previous time.

Hastily and eagerly, her hand travelled down to his pants and unbuttoned his trousers. He groaned when she took his manhood into her hand. It felt warm and hard, and she felt it beading with wetness.

"Charlotte..." she heard him say against her lips, and it drove her wild with desire.

Lifting herself up just slightly, without breaking the kiss, she adjusted his manhood, pressing it to her swollen bud. It slid up and down so easily, and she could feel herself between her fingers, spreading that wet heat.

He groaned again, louder this time, when she slowly slid down onto him, taking him inside of her.

"I want you..." she managed to murmur as he kept kissing her.

Her words seemed to awaken something inside of him. He took her by the waist and started thrusting up into her, deep and hard, forcing the very breath out of her lungs.

She kept taking him into her mindlessly, feeling that tidal wave of pleasure nearing the final point of no return. Wet and wild with desire, she gripped him, biting his lip, moaning loudly as she stared into his eyes. She didn't want to look away for a single moment while she was claiming him.

Finally, he thrust one more time, and a million little stars exploded in her field of vision, while ecstasy filled every fibre of her being. He followed suit a moment later, and they remained like that, lost in the throttle of pleasure for a few breathless moments.

Charlotte stepped back first, smoothing her skirt with trembling fingers.

"I should go," she said quietly, gathering herself. "There is much to prepare before tomorrow."

She turned toward the door. Cassian's hand closed around her wrist in a way a drowning man might seize a lifeline.

"Will you come to me tonight?" he asked.

She kept her back to him for a heartbeat. Then, gently, she slipped her hand free and faced him.

"I will, but only for convenience, not affection," she clarified. "I am honouring the terms of our marriage. You made them very clear."

He didn't say anything, so she continued. "I will not ask for things you do not wish to give, like your heart. But I *am* your wife. And if there is physical affection to be had between us," she swallowed, lifting her chin, "then I am willing, but without nonsense emotions to complicate matters."

Cassian went rigid.

"Is that what you want?" he asked.

She met his gaze without wavering. "Yes. We both have needs, Cassian. And that is all I require. Nothing more."

Then she opened the door and walked out. Cassian didn't follow. But Charlotte felt his gaze burning into her back as she left. She knew, with a pang she refused to acknowledge aloud, that she had hurt him.

Worse, she had hurt herself.

Chapter Twenty-Five

The letter went out at dawn, stating that she wanted to meet Edmund at the port on Sunday evening, at exactly 8 pm.

Cassian watched from a shadowed alcove across the narrow street. The brim of his hat was pulled low, and his greatcoat blended into the morning fog. Nicholas stood a short distance away, and two of Cassian's most trusted men were stationed at opposite corners of the lane, all in plain clothing. No one looking on would recognize a duke, his brother-in-law, or a guard. They were merely figures among market-goers and errand boys.

Charlotte, cloaked and veiled, approached the old apothecary with measured steps. Cassian tracked her every moment. She looked composed as she slipped down the side lane toward the rear post alcove. That hidden nook had once been her secret place where, in her innocence, she had left letters for Edmund's unseen associate.

Never again, Cassian vowed silently. *Not on my watch.*

Charlotte crouched, slid the folded letter into the crevice beneath the loose stone, and rose with a calm, practiced motion. Only Cassian, who had come to know every shift in her expression, would have noticed the flicker of emotion beneath her veil. She turned to leave.

Charlotte and her maid disappeared into the carriage, and only when the wheels began to roll did Cassian finally allow himself to exhale. The letter lay hidden in the crevice behind the apothecary, just as it had in the past. The trap was set.

Nicholas stepped up beside him, adjusting his coat against the morning chill. "You watched her like a hawk," he murmured.

Cassian did not bother to deny it. "If Edmund still has eyes in this town, I will not risk him setting his gaze on her again."

Nicholas nodded once. "I've men stationed at both ends of the lane. If anyone checks the hiding place, we'll know. And when they make a move toward the port, we follow."

Cassian's jaw tightened. "Edmund must take the bait. There will not be another chance."

Without another word, they left the alleyway and mounted their horses. They rode in silence until Nicholas broke it.

"You disapprove of the plan," he said quietly. "Still."

Cassian kept his eyes on the road ahead. "She should not have been involved."

"She insisted," Nicholas reminded him. "And she is not wrong. This will flush him out faster than waiting on rumours."

Cassian gripped the reins a fraction tighter.

Nicholas observed him a moment longer, then sighed. "You are not merely angry. You are afraid."

Cassian shot him a hard look. "I do not fear Edmund Larke."

"No," Nicholas said calmly. "You fear losing my sister."

Cassian looked away at anything but the truth laid bare between them.

"When Edmund is caught," Cassian said at last, "this ends, for her and for all of us."

Nicholas offered no argument. There was nothing more to say. They rode on. Soon enough, they reached Duskbourne Hall and together made their way down the corridor toward Cassian's study. A footman bowed as they passed, and the butler stepped forward to ask whether tea should be brought, but Cassian dismissed him with a curt shake of the head.

When they reached his study, Cassian pushed open the door and strode inside. Nicholas followed, closing it firmly behind them.

Cassian froze after only two steps. Something was wrong.

His desk looked unchanged at first glance: neat stacks of correspondence, ink stand aligned, quills trimmed and clean. But one of the small drawers on the right side hung open by a hair's breadth.

Cassian's pulse sharpened. *I locked that.*

He crossed the room in three long strides and tugged the drawer fully open. Inside, ledgers and sealed documents lay slightly askew, as though someone had thumbed through them and attempted to set them back in order... *almost* successfully.

Nicholas came to his side. "Duskbourne?"

He didn't answer. He had already noticed something else, a ledger on the desk that he distinctly remembered putting away before leaving that morning. Its pages were ruffled, as though someone had rifled through it in haste.

Cassian flipped the ledger open. A small slip of paper fluttered out and fell onto the polished wood.

Nicholas lifted it before Cassian could.

The message was only five words, scrawled in an arrogant, jagged hand:

Not as blind as you.

Nicholas swore under his breath. "He was here."

Cassian took the note, gripping it so tightly it nearly tore. Edmund Larke had walked into *his home,* into *Charlotte's home.*

"He is taunting you," Nicholas said quietly. "Taunting us both."

Cassian moved to the fireplace, knuckles white around the paper. "No. He is testing *me.* Testing how close he can come and how far he can push before I strike. He knows now that he can never have Charlotte, and he is determined to ruin her. But I won't let that happen."

He tossed the note into the flames and watched it curl, blacken, and vanish. The fire hissed, and anger roared in him, hotter than the blaze.

"He has been in these rooms," Cassian growled. "Touching our books, our ledgers, our *life.*" His fists clenched. "Testing defences is the act of a man planning more."

Nicholas's voice dropped. "And Charlotte?"

Cassian exhaled slowly, the question cutting deeper than any insult Edmund could craft.

Charlotte was the target. The bait. The *obsession.*

And now Edmund had breached the walls of Duskbourne itself.

"I will find him," Cassian said. "And I will end this. We tighten the watch and double the guards. And Larke will learn that he has made the gravest mistake of his life."

Cassian would hunt him without mercy, not because of duty, not even for justice. But because the man had dared to threaten what Cassian could no longer lie to himself about:

Charlotte mattered... more than anything.

***

The afternoon sun filtered warmly through the tall windows of Duskbourne, but Charlotte found no warmth in it. The manor felt stifling. It was thick with silence, secrets, and the memory of Cassian's unreadable eyes. She needed air, something that belonged to *her* and not to the fear curling in every corridor.

She slipped into her riding habit, tied her bonnet, and made her way to the stables. The grooms looked surprised to see her alone.

"Shall I fetch a guard, my lady?" one asked.

"That won't be necessary," Charlotte replied, offering a polite smile. "I won't be long. Just a short ride on the grounds."

The man hesitated, but she was a duchess, and one never questioned a duchess. He saddled her horse without any further comments.

Moments later, Charlotte was astride her mare, guiding the animal through the familiar paths of Duskbourne territory. The wind against her face eased her breath, and the rhythmic motion of the ride soothed her frayed pride and wounded heart.

She told herself she needed only half an hour, perhaps even less. She would not stray far. She followed a less-travelled trail lined with old trees, their branches arching overhead to form a living tunnel of green. Sunlight dappled the path. Leaves whispered softly with each breeze.

For a time, she began to feel calm again… until she heard it.

Charlotte slowed her horse, glancing back over her shoulder, but saw no one. She exhaled.

A deer, perhaps.

Or a stable boy returning from patrol. Or the wind. Always, it could be the wind.

As she was resting, taking in the sight, she heard another sound, only closer this time. It was a branch snapping.

She turned sharply in her saddle, her eyes surveying the line of trees. The shadows were thick there, resembling long fingers stretching across the ground. Nothing moved. There was no servant in sight and no animal that she could see.

And yet, she could feel it, that prickling on the back of her neck and the sensation of being watched.

"Do not be foolish," she whispered to herself. "It is only nerves. Perhaps a fox or dog in the underbrush."

She clicked her tongue and set her mare into a brisk trot. But the sensation did not vanish. In fact, it intensified. At a bend in the trail, she risked another look, and her breath stopped.

Between two trees, half-hidden by shadow, stood a figure. When he moved slightly to the left, she recognized him.

"Edmund!" she gasped his name.

His coat was travel-worn, and his face was thinner and sharper than she remembered. But his eyes, which she once mistook for soulful, now burned with obsession and rage.

"Charlotte," he said, stepping into her path. "Finally. I knew you'd come."

She felt her pulse lurch. "You have no right to be here. Leave at once."

He ignored the command, stepping forward. "We must speak about the letters, about everything," he rushed out. "I know you don't mean what you've done. You're frightened and confused, and your husband has twisted you against me. But you love me. You wrote it with your own hand."

"No." Her voice was ice. "Those letters are nothing now. You tricked me. You lied. And you will not use my words against me again."

His jaw twitched. "Then come with me. Just for an hour. There is a coach waiting beyond the south field. We can leave before anyone notices—"

Charlotte recoiled, pulling her horse back. "I will not go anywhere with you. Remove yourself from my path and leave before you make this worse."

His desperation sharpened. "You don't understand. If you deny me now, you ruin me. Everything I planned and everything I endured will have been for nothing. You owe me that conversation. You *owe* me an explanation."

"I owe you nothing," she snapped. "Now step aside."

Edmund's eyes darkened. In two bold strides, he reached for her reins.

Charlotte jerked them away. "Unhand me!"

"Charlotte, please, just hear me—"

"I said release me!" she shouted, with her voice ringing through the trees.

Edmund glanced over his shoulder, and there was paranoia flashing in his gaze. "Lower your voice," he hissed. "If anyone hears—"

Charlotte saw it then, clearly, without the blinding haze of the past: Edmund had never been charming, nor poetic, nor misunderstood. He was *dangerous.*

"I will ride back to the house," she said, gathering her reins. "If you follow me, I will scream until the entire estate comes running."

His face twisted. "You will *not* leave me again!"

He moved suddenly, grabbing for her horse's bridle. The mare, startled, reared violently. Charlotte gasped, clutching at the saddle, but the jolt was too sharp and the angle too steep.

"Stop! Edmund, stop!"

The horse bucked. And Charlotte was thrown. She hit the ground hard and felt the air knocked from her lungs. Pain flared across her hip and shoulder. The world spun for a moment, but when she blinked, Edmund was leaning over her.

"Charlotte—"

"Stay away from me," she spat.

Before she could dodge, Edmund seized her wrist and yanked her toward him. Charlotte twisted, fighting him, nails raking across his hand. He hissed in pain but only tightened his grip.

"Let go!" she cried, striking his arm, his shoulder, anything she could reach.

But Edmund had come prepared. From his coat, he drew a length of coarse rope. Charlotte's blood went cold.

"No, no, you will not—" she gasped, thrashing with every ounce of strength she had.

Her struggle was fierce, but she had been winded by the fall. Edmund overpowered her, dragging her arms behind her back. The rope bit into her wrists as he tied the knot. Charlotte bucked and kicked, but he shoved her forward until she stumbled off-balance.

"Stop fighting me!" he panted. "You are making this harder."

"And you are insane!" she spat. "Cassian will find me. And when he does, you will pay for this."

He looked like he wanted to say something, but stubborn madness smothered it.

"Walk," he ordered, jerking her forward by the arm.

Charlotte stumbled over a root but steadied herself. Her mind raced. While Edmund dragged her onward, she memorized everything around her, from rocks clustered in uneven patches of ground and branches half-buried in moss, to birdsong and the fact that she was too far away from the house for anyone to hear her scream.

She cast a glance at Edmund's coat pocket, at the trees, at the brush, searching for anything.

There was no escape.

Chapter Twenty-Six

Cassian needed to find Charlotte now. Edmund Larke was inside Duskbourne, and no locked door was safe any longer.

Charlotte needed to know. She needed to be warned. She needed to be protected.

He strode to her sitting room first, but it was empty. Then, he checked the morning parlour. It was also empty. He checked the terrace, the gallery, even the library where she often escaped to read alone, with the same result.

Cassian's urgency sharpened into unease. At last, he found Miriam holding a stack of linens in her arms. Cassian approached her in three swift strides.

"Miriam," he inquired, "where is your mistress? I must speak with her at once."

The maid seemed startled by his intensity. "Your Grace, Her Grace went riding."

Cold spread through Cassian's veins.

"Riding?" he repeated slowly. "Alone?"

Miriam faltered. "She said she wished for air and would go only around the grounds. She promised to return quickly. It has only been... well, over an hour now. She said she would be back in half that."

Cassian closed his eyes, feeling fury and dread coursing through him in equal measure.

She was alone after Edmund stood in these walls.

He opened his eyes again, sharper than steel. "Listen to me carefully," he said. "Charlotte is in danger, whether she realizes it or not. Edmund Larke has breached the manor. We must assume he is still nearby."

Miriam gasped, colour draining from her face. "Your Grace..."

"Her brother is in my study; inform him of it immediately," Cassian ordered. "Tell him to send word for my best men, no more than five, and do so quietly. If Edmund is on the grounds, I will not have panic or rumour driving him deeper into the shadows."

Miriam bobbed a shaky curtsy and fled. Cassian didn't wait.

When he reached the stables, he barked an order before the stablemaster could even bow. "My horse. Now."

Within moments, Cassian was mounted, with reins tight in his fists. At that moment, Nicholas arrived.

"Miriam told me everything," he said breathlessly.

"Charlotte rode out alone," Cassian echoed. "I'll take the eastern paths. You take the ridge. Send two men to sweep the south fields and one to the old orchard. No one rides alone except me." Cassian met Nicholas's gaze. "He wants her, Nicholas. And if he has seen her—"

He didn't finish. He didn't have to.

Nicholas nodded once. "Bring her home. I'll cover the rest."

Cassian spurred his stallion forward. The farther he rode, the more the woods thickened, with branches clawing at his coat as though nature itself were trying to slow him. Then, suddenly, he heard the thunder of hooves. Cassian reined in sharply just as a horse burst through the trees ahead, riderless, wild-eyed, and lathered with sweat.

It was Charlotte's mare.

Cassian's heart stopped.

"Easy," he murmured, catching the bridle as the frightened mare danced sideways. The animal trembled beneath his hand.

Something happened... something violent.

He released the reins, gave the horse a firm slap on the flank, and sent it galloping back toward the manor, away from danger. Then he turned his stallion in the direction the mare had fled from.

He found signs almost immediately. A snapped branch led to a glove crushed into the earth. There were hoof marks scattered in panicked circles, and on the ground, a patch of churned soil as though two people struggled there.

Cassian dismounted in one fluid motion and knelt. His fingers brushed the disturbed ground. He could see the imprint of a boot heel not belonging to Charlotte. It was male.

Edmund.

Cassian straightened slowly. His pulse was no longer racing. It was pounding, brutal, and steady, like a war drum.

"She fell," he whispered, seeing scuffed earth where knees and palms had dug in. "And he took her on foot."

He spun, scanning the tree line. Branches broke in a path leading east, toward the thickest part of the woods and, beyond that, the southern fields.

Cassian mounted again, dug in his heels, and shot forward. He would follow every footprint, every crushed blade of grass, every snapped twig until it led him to Charlotte. He rode like a madman, like a man who had nothing and everything to lose, until he finally burst through the last line of trees and into a clearing.

What he saw turned his blood to fire.

Edmund was dragging Charlotte by the arm, her hands bound. Her dress was torn at the sleeve, and she was stumbling against the uneven ground as she struggled to resist him.

Cassian's pulse roared in his ears.

"Edmund!" he bellowed, allowing his voice to ring through the clearing.

Both Edmund and Charlotte whipped around. For one suspended heartbeat, they stared at each other: predator and prey, hunter and target.

Edmund's expression twisted. "Stay back!" he shouted, pulling Charlotte against him as a shield. "She is mine! She *chose* me!"

Cassian's reply was a growl. "Release. Her. Now."

Charlotte seized that moment. She stomped her heel down hard on Edmund's boot. Edmund cursed, loosening his grip. Cassian was already off his horse and charging.

The two men collided with brutal force. Cassian struck first, slamming Edmund back against a tree. Edmund scrambled, looking wild and desperate, swinging wildly. Cassian ducked the clumsy strike and drove his fist into Edmund's ribs once, then twice, until Edmund gasped for breath.

"You dare touch my wife?" Cassian snarled, seizing Edmund by the collar and slamming him to the ground.

Edmund clawed at him, spitting frantic words. "She was mine! She loved me! She—!"

"Liar!" Cassian roared, landing a final punch that sent Edmund sprawling, stunned and gasping in the dirt. "You preyed on her. You used her. And now you will answer for it."

As Cassian pinned Edmund, Charlotte moved with sharp purpose. She darted to the edge of the clearing. With her hands still bound, she pressed her wrists against a sharp branch, sawing and twisting until the rope frayed. The moment it snapped, she ran back, grabbing the fallen rope and handing it to Cassian.

Cassian wrenched Edmund's arms behind his back and tied the knots with trained, merciless precision. Edmund fought weakly, still swearing and kicking, cursing both Charlotte's and Cassian's names, but the struggle was finished. He was beaten, bound, and no longer a threat.

Cassian hauled him upright and forced him back against a tree, tying the rope once more around the trunk to ensure he could not run.

Edmund glared at them both, madness still flickering in his eyes. "This is not done," he spat. "You think marriage makes her yours? She will never—"

Cassian silenced him with a cold, deadly stare. "You have lost. You have no claim. Charlotte owes you nothing."

Charlotte stepped forward then. "I do not fear you anymore, Edmund," she said.

For the first time, Edmund faltered. The last of his leverage, his fantasy, his control... it slipped from him, visibly and irrevocably.

Cassian turned to Charlotte, cupping her face with his hands. "Are you hurt?"

She shook her head, though her breath still trembled. "Only shaken."

He wanted to kiss her, to take her into his arms and never let go, but he couldn't. Instead, he looked at Edmund again. "The law will take you now, and I will personally ensure it keeps you."

Edmund didn't say anything to that. His face was twisted in furious defeat.

At that very moment, a few of the guards arrived, and Cassian instructed them to take him back to the manor house, where he would wait for the arrival of the constables. Whatever other crimes he had committed, along with staining Charlotte's name and threatening to kidnap her, would keep him locked up.

Then, Cassian slipped an arm around Charlotte, steadying her as he led her toward the horse. The danger had passed, but Cassian's pulse had not yet slowed. He lifted Charlotte carefully into the saddle, settling her in front of him on his stallion. Her hands trembled as they gripped the pommel, and without hesitation, he wrapped one arm securely around her waist, anchoring her to him.

"Lean back," he murmured.

She did. Her head rested against his shoulder, and the moment he felt the weight of her, something inside him cracked wide open. Cassian clicked his tongue, urging the horse forward at a calm pace, keeping her close.

Then, he heard her whisper. "I thought I might not make it back..."

Cassian closed his eyes briefly, and the words tore through him. "Do not say such a thing."

"It's true," she whispered. "For a moment, I thought..." her voice cracked. "I thought I would never see you again."

He tightened his hold around her, pulling her back against his chest. "You will always come back to me," he whispered back. "Not because of chance or the perfect moment, but because I will move heaven and earth to make it so."

Charlotte drew in a trembling breath and turned slightly toward him. "Cassian..."

He looked down at her, at those blue eyes still shimmering with fear, and everything he had held back fell to ash.

"I cannot lose you, Charlotte," he confessed. "Today I realized something I should have known long ago. I want you... *all* of you. Not only in the dark, not only in stolen moments. I want your mornings, your laughter, your stubborn opinions. I want every part you have to give."

Cassian lifted a hand, brushing a stray lock of hair from her cheek with aching tenderness.

"I am in love with you," he said. "And I will not pretend otherwise for one more hour."

Her lips parted, but no words came. She turned forward again, but she leaned into him fully this time, her body melting against his, and her fingers curling over his forearm as though anchoring herself to the truth she had longed to hear. Cassian rested his cheek briefly against her hair.

The road stretched before them, winding toward home, but for the first time since their wedding, Cassian felt that *home* was not a place.

It was the woman in his arms.

Chapter Twenty-Seven

Morning light spilled cheerfully through the tall windows of the Duskbourne library, turning dust motes into dancing flecks of gold. Charlotte stood at the long mahogany table, sorting through a stack of correspondence that seemed determined to multiply, no matter how diligently she worked. Cassian, for his part, was meant to be assisting her.

Meant to.

At present, he appeared far more occupied with mischief than organization.

"You are not even pretending to help," Charlotte remarked, narrowing her eyes at him as she folded a letter and placed it neatly into a pile. "I have seen more earnest effort from baby Augustus when he attempts to eat his boot."

Cassian lounged in one of the leather chairs, entirely unrepentant. "Boot leather is very compelling to a child. These letters, however, are unforgivably dull."

She pouted. "They are only dull because you refuse to open a single one."

"I opened one," he objected.

"You read the address and handed it back to me."

Cassian rose with a dramatic sigh and reached for another sheet. But instead of reading it, he raised a brow, tucked it behind his back, and stepped away from the table.

Charlotte froze. "Cassian Oberon, do not dare."

He smiled *that* smile, the one that made him look younger, sharper, and entirely too handsome for her sanity. "If you want this letter, you must retrieve it."

She stared at him, looking utterly yet playfully scandalized. "We are not children."

"No," he agreed solemnly, "but I suspect you are just as competitive as one."

He turned, placing himself deliberately out of reach. Charlotte's laughter escaped before she could smother it.

"You are impossible."

"And you are avoiding pursuit," he taunted.

Charlotte lifted her chin with mock dignity, circled the table, and made a daring lunge for the letter. Cassian dodged her, swift and delighted, slipping between chairs as though evading her in this library were his life's calling. She nearly caught his coat before he pivoted again, entirely too nimble for a duke who claimed to be exhausted by paperwork.

At last, she cornered him near the hearth.

"Hand it over," she demanded, breathless and laughing.

"Never."

In response, she seized the nearest scrap of paper from the table and flicked it smartly against his shoulder. "There. Consider that your warning shot."

Cassian's eyes widened with playful outrage. "You assaulted me with stationery."

"And I shall do it again," she threatened, lifting another page.

"Charlotte," he said, advancing on her with that wicked glint in his eye, "if you strike me once more, I will be forced to retaliate, and I assure you, I can be far more devious than you."

She brandished the paper nonetheless. "I welcome the challenge."

Their laughter echoed across the vaulted ceiling, dissolving the shadows that had haunted them only days before. The Edmund ordeal, the sleepless nights, and the bruised fears fell away.

Cassian stopped, the teasing slowly softening into something quieter. He stepped closer, close enough that she felt the warmth of him even through her gown.

"You laugh beautifully," he murmured.

Charlotte, suddenly aware of her breath and the scandalous nearness between them, lowered her gaze. "I had nearly forgotten how."

"Then we must ensure you never forget again."

Cassian slid his hands to her waist, pulling her closer to himself. Her pulse was a wild, breathless flutter. His dark eyes searched hers as though he could read every hidden thought she had ever tried to bury.

"And I find," he murmured, "that I want to be the reason you continue to smile... every morning, every day, every year we have."

Her breath caught. One teasing moment had become something entirely different. He caged her gently between the hearth and his own body. His hands settled on her hips with a confidence that made her knees weaken.

"Cassian..." she whispered.

The teasing was gone. The laughter was gone. What remained between them was heat, raw and long denied.

He lowered his head, brushing his lips against hers in the faintest, most devastating ghost of a kiss.

"Tell me to stop," he breathed.

She didn't. Instead, Charlotte surged forward and kissed him. The world dissolved. Cassian answered her with a hunger that stole the strength from her legs. His mouth moved against hers with urgency and reverence both, as though kissing her was not desire alone but a vow. She fisted her hands in his coat, pulling him closer, needing him nearer still.

Somehow, they sank to the library floor. She did not know whether he pulled her down with him or whether she took him there herself. All she knew was heat, and the press of his body, and the dizzying rush of being wholly, finally wanted.

He kissed her again and again, deeper, slower, then desperate once more. He lay her down, grabbing one of the pillows from the chaise lounge for her head. His tenderness almost made her chuckle, but the heat of the moment prevented her from doing so.

Desperately, he pooled her skirt around her waist, unable to wait a single moment. The need to feel him inside of her was immense. Although she was new to lovemaking, she felt that each time, she wanted him more, if such a thing were even possible.

Desire took hold of them both as he found her wet heat ready for him. Her hair pins now lay scattered on the Axminster, and as she looked deeply into his eyes, she knew that she could not love him more.

She gripped him tighter, demanding more of him. Her lips crashed against his, love merging with desire in a glorious sensation that was seizing her completely. This was what she wanted, what she yearned for: to be completely and fully his, mind, body, and soul.

He kept taking her, claiming her deeper and deeper, and she became mindless with desire. Her body clenched around him, feeling him throbbing deep inside of her, as ecstasy rocked them both into oblivion.

They breathed loudly together, drinking in each other's air, while she felt his heart pounding. She had never experienced such a rush of emotions, sensations, such a pinnacle of delight that made her dissolve in his arms. He bucked against her, filling her with his seed.

When he pulled away, her cheeks were flushed, but she didn't mind. She watched him with an adoring gaze, always managing to find a new tenderness about him, about the man who didn't even know what tenderness was.

Suddenly, he cupped her chin and turned her face toward him. "Charlotte... I... love you."

Time stopped. She stared at him, with her lips parted and her heart pounding so hard it almost hurt. Cassian now cupped her entire face in his hands, and there was no shield left in him. There was no distance and no mask, only truth.

"I love you," he said again, steadier this time, as though he needed her to feel it to believe it. "All of you. And I will spend the rest of my life proving it, if you let me."

Tears stung her eyes, and they were impossible to hold back. She framed his face with both hands and kissed him once more. Letting her heart speak through the softness of her lips. When she drew back, her voice trembled, but her certainty did not.

"I love you, Cassian, entirely and helplessly. And I think I did long before I dared admit it."

A shaky breath escaped him, and he pulled her into his arms, holding her as though she were something both precious and powerful. They stayed there on the library floor, tangled together. The shadows no longer felt heavy. The silence no longer felt cold.

Charlotte finally exhaled in peace. This warmth, this devotion, this love was theirs. And it had finally been spoken.

***

It was several weeks later that Charlotte returned from the physician in town. Her hands lay clasped tightly in her lap, though she could not keep them still. Excitement fluttered in her chest as though joy itself were trying to take flight inside her.

Pregnant.

The word felt unreal, sacred, terrifying, and wondrous all at once.

A child. Their child.

She pressed a hand to her stomach, where new life had already begun. The physician had spoken gently, smiling as he offered his congratulations, and Charlotte had smiled back, though tears had threatened to spill. She could already imagine Cassian holding a tiny hand, or resting his palm against her growing belly, or lifting their son or daughter into the air with laughter in his eyes.

By the time the carriage pulled into Duskbourne's courtyard, she was nearly trembling with the warm anticipation of sharing the news.

She found Cassian in his study.

He stood by the desk, sorting through estate documents, not noticing her at first. At the sight of her, his expression softened until he truly looked at her. She must have been glowing or nervous or too breathless by half, for his posture straightened immediately.

"Charlotte?" he asked. "What is it? Are you unwell?"

She shook her head, suddenly shy. "No. I am..." Her voice faltered. This moment mattered. She drew in a steady breath and stepped toward him. "Cassian, I have just come from the physician. He has confirmed something I suspected these past weeks."

His eyes searched hers. She could see concern, curiosity, and a shadow of fear.

Charlotte reached for his hand. "I am with child."

Cassian's hand went cold in hers. His expression changed. She expected to see joy, not horror and anguish. His posture stiffened. His jaw clenched, and he appeared almost angry.

"Cassian?" she asked softly.

He took a step back, letting go of her hand.

"I... see," he said at last. His voice was flat.

Charlotte blinked, confusion now slicing through her earlier joy. "I thought you would be pleased. Or at least," she swallowed, "*something.*"

Cassian ran a hand through his hair, turning away from her as though he needed distance simply to breathe. "It is... a great responsibility," he managed. "There is much to think about, much to prepare. I need time."

Time.

The word stung more than a shout would have.

"You are not happy," Charlotte whispered.

He closed his eyes. "I did not say that."

"You did not have to." Her voice trembled despite her efforts to steady it.

Cassian exhaled in a breath that was long and strained. "Charlotte, please. I am trying—"

"To what?" she asked. "Feel nothing?"

He turned then, and the torment in his eyes was unmistakable, but it was not the kind that welcomed comfort. It was the kind that shut doors. Charlotte knew that look. She had seen shades of it before, when the past crept up on him and stole him away from the present.

He spoke with heavy effort. "I need... a moment alone."

And though the words were measured, they struck clean through her. Charlotte looked at him, at this man she loved, who loved her, and yet now seemed oceans away when they should have been the closest.

"As you wish," she said quietly.

She left the study with her head held high, but her steps grew unsteady the moment she was out of sight.

In the corridor, she pressed a hand against her stomach again, not joyful now, but protective. She understood Cassian carried ghosts. But for the first time, she feared those ghosts might steal something from them she could not bear to lose.

Charlotte barely remembered the walk from Cassian's study to the front steps. Her vision blurred, her throat burned, and her heartbeat crashed against her ribs like a desperate fist. By the time she reached the entrance hall, she could no longer pretend composure. She only knew she could not remain there.

Her carriage had not yet been dismissed. The footman stood beside it, awaiting further instruction.

"Your Grace?" he asked, startled by her haste and pallor.

"Take me to Hawthorne House," Charlotte demanded. "At once."

He hesitated only long enough to bow. "Yes, Your Grace."

Within moments, she was inside the carriage, the door shut behind her. As the wheels lurched into motion, Charlotte pressed both hands to her mouth, fighting the sob that broke through anyway. She had imagined Cassian lifting her, spinning her, perhaps even kissing her with laughter in his eyes when she told him the news.

She had pictured joy, but instead she had seen fear and withdrawal.

By the time the carriage stopped in front of Hawthorne House, Charlotte's eyes were raw, and her heart was aching so fiercely she thought it might split. The butler ushered her inside without question and sent for Lydia at once.

She appeared moments later in the drawing room. One look at Charlotte's face and her expression changed to alarm.

"Charlotte, good heavens, what has happened?"

That single question undid the last of her composure. Charlotte rushed forward, and Lydia caught her, pulling her into a fierce embrace. The dam broke. Charlotte wept against her shoulder, clinging to her as though she might drown otherwise.

When at last the sobs quieted, Lydia guided her to the settee and poured her tea with gentle hands.

"Tell me," Lydia urged. "All of it."

Charlotte wiped her cheeks and drew a shaky breath. "Lydia... I am with child."

Lydia's gasp was delighted. "Charlotte, that is wonderful news! Why are you—" She stopped, her eyes narrowing at the conclusion. "What did the Duke say?"

Charlotte stared down at her clasped hands. "He... did not say much at all."

Lydia waited.

"It was as if I had delivered a burden instead of a blessing," Charlotte whispered. "He went still. He stepped back from me, Lydia, as though I had *frightened* him."

"Oh, Charlotte." Lydia reached for her hand.

"I know he loves me," Charlotte continued, her voice on the verge of breaking. "I *know* it. But he shut himself off as if joy itself were a danger, as if my happiness were something he could not bear to touch." Tears spilled again. "He used to come to me with passion, with warmth, with desire. And now, when I give him the greatest joy I ever could..." She swallowed. "He looked at me as though I had doomed us both."

Lydia squeezed her hand tightly. "You have done nothing wrong. Cassian's reaction is not a reflection of you nor of this child. It is his fear speaking."

Charlotte closed her eyes. "But how am I to raise a child with a man who flinches at the idea of loving it?"

Lydia pulled her into another embrace. "You will not face this alone. And Cassian will have to face his past if he wishes to deserve you and this baby. But for now, rest. Let yourself feel what you feel. You are safe here."

Charlotte leaned into her, exhausted and unravelling. She had a right to want joy and a right to demand a future not haunted by ghosts.

And if Casian truly loved her, he would have to prove it.

Chapter Twenty-Eight

Charlotte had avoided the west wing for months.

She avoided it after the wedding, even after trust and affection had begun to blossom. That wing with the shuttered corridor sealed by Cassian's grief, remained a place she approached only in thought, never in step.

But today, something drew her there. Perhaps instinct, perhaps hope, perhaps the stubborn seed of love that refused to wilt.

The corridor was dim and hushed, and dust motes were swirling in pale ribbons of morning light. As she neared the doorway she had once foolishly forced open, she heard movement inside.

Her pulse stuttered. Charlotte paused at the threshold by the door that had been left ajar and watched silently for a moment.

Cassian stood in the centre of the old room with his sleeves rolled. He was carefully lifting items from a shelf: a ribbon, a small silver rattle, a folded quilt. He examined each one before placing it reverently into a wooden trunk at his feet.

She hesitated to step forward. After all, they hadn't spoken in days, since she had told him about her pregnancy. She wondered if she should interrupt him or let him have his moment.

At last, she stepped forward.

"What are you doing?" she asked softly, wanting to know, to be a part of his heart.

Cassian turned. Surprise flickered across his face, followed by a gentler emotion. She felt relief. At least he was not upset with her.

"Charlotte," he said quietly. "I did not hear you."

She hesitated, eyes drifting to the objects in the trunk. "I thought you never wished to enter this room again."

He looked around slowly. "Nor did I... not then." His hand brushed the windowsill, clearing a line through the dust. "But now... things have changed."

Charlotte moved closer, her voice barely above a whisper. "Because of the baby."

Cassian nodded.

"For so long," he said, choosing his words with care, "this room has been... a grave I never buried. I could not bring myself to move anything. It felt like erasing them: my wife, my son, even the hope I once had." His throat worked, and Charlotte's heart tightened at the rawness in his voice. "I feared that if I touched any of it, I would break."

She reached out, lightly resting her fingertips on the corner of the trunk. "And now?"

Cassian drew a breath. This was the most vulnerable she had ever seen him, and she didn't want to frighten him by demanding more words than he was ready to give. So she remained silent and waiting. "Now I fear something different. I fear losing you and our child." His voice cracked, but only for a moment. "The last time I loved this deeply, I buried everything that mattered. I swore I would never risk that grief again. When you told me you were expecting, the memory returned so violently I could scarcely breathe."

Charlotte swallowed, realizing that it was never about him not loving their child, but about loving it too much, and fearing for it.

"Cassian..."

"I reacted shamefully," he continued. "Not because I do not want this child, but because I do. I want it more than I ever allowed myself to want anything again. And that terrified me."

Cassian stepped closer, not touching her yet as though awaiting permission.

"I do not want this room to remain frozen in sorrow," he said. "We will move these keepsakes elsewhere with honour, not neglect. And this..." His gaze swept the faded curtains, the empty cradle, and the dust-covered toys. "This will become a nursery again, for *our* child, filled with light and laughter instead of ghosts."

Charlotte's breath trembled. Slowly, she lifted her hand to his cheek. He closed his eyes at the touch, leaning into it like a man starved for warmth.

"I was afraid," she whispered, "that my joy became your burden."

Cassian opened his eyes, anguish and devotion shining equally in them. "Never. Your joy is my salvation. I simply... needed a moment to learn how to carry it."

Something inside Charlotte unclenched, something that had been wound tight since she left for Lydia's. She stepped into his arms, and this time, he held her without armour or fear of being seen.

They stood like that for a long breath, the soft hush of the abandoned nursery wrapping around them like a blanket.

Cassian's thumb brushed over her knuckles, and Charlotte leaned into him, resting her head lightly against his shoulder.

After a time, he spoke. "Have you thought of names?"

Charlotte smiled, the question warming her from the inside out. "A few."

Cassian drew her toward the window seat, and they sank down together, close enough that their knees touched. He kept her hand in his.

"Go on, then," he said. "Tell me what my child shall be called."

She laughed softly. "*Our* child, Cassian."

He inclined his head gently. "*Our* child."

Charlotte considered. "For a girl... Eleanor is beautiful. And meaningful. But I don't wish to reopen wounds."

Cassian shook his head gently. "No. Not that name, although it is beautiful. Some memories should rest." He squeezed her hand. "Choose one that is only ours."

"Then perhaps... Clara? Or Amelia? Or Rose?" she suggested with a shy hopefulness in her voice.

Cassian smiled. "Clara Oberon. I confess, I like the sound."

"And if it is a boy?" she asked.

He huffed a faint laugh. "I suppose there must be a Cassian the Second someday."

She nudged him. "Someday, perhaps, but not this one. He deserves a name of his own. What of William? Or Philip?"

Cassian paused. "Philip," he repeated, testing it. "Strong... steady. Yes. Philip... I could see that."

They fell into soft laughter then, imagining a child with her smile or his stubborn brow, a nursery filled with mischief and light, and light footsteps echoing in the very hall that had once echoed with silence.

For the first time, their future did not feel fragile. It felt possible.

Cassian released her hand only long enough to reach into his coat. "There is something else." He drew out a small, leather-bound book tied with a ribbon. "For you. I ordered it weeks ago, and it arrived yesterday."

Charlotte blinked. "What is it?"

"Open and see."

She undid the ribbon and lifted the cover. Her breath caught. *Persuasion.* It was her favourite, one she had mentioned only once, in passing, during a late-night conversation in the library.

"You remembered," she whispered.

Cassian's expression softened. "I remember everything you say, especially when you speak of the things that shaped you."

Speechless, she smoothed her hand over the first page.

"May I?" he asked, nodding to the book.

She gave it to him, unable to hide her delight. Cassian turned to a marked passage and began reading in a low, steady voice. The words flowed like quiet poetry through the dim room. It was a passage about steadfast love, not loud or flamboyant, but constant, enduring, and true.

"I can listen no longer in silence. I must speak to you by such means as are within my reach. You pierce my soul. I am half agony, half hope. Tell me not that I am too late... I offer myself

to you again with a heart even more your own than when you almost broke it, eight years and a half ago."

Charlotte listened, and her heart felt full. However, it was not because of Austen's words, for she herself had read them a dozen times, but because of *his;* because Cassian had chosen this passage, this story, and this moment to offer her peace. He wanted to pledge to her, without theatrics or any spectacle, that he was here *with* her and *for* her.

When he finished, she lay her head on his shoulder once more. He rested his cheek against her hair. No danger threatened in that moment. No ghosts prowled. No fear choked the air.

There was only sunlight on dust motes, the warmth of his hand in hers, and the promise of a future they would face together one step, one breath, one heartbeat at a time.

Epilogue

Cassian had never known a morning so endless.

Dawn had barely crested the horizon, yet his nerves were stretched so tightly that every sound in Duskbourne sent his pulse leaping. Each one made him stop, listen, and brace himself for news.

He paced the nursery again, his tenth or twelfth circuit, in a futile effort to straighten what needed no straightening. The midwife's satchel sat upon the table: linen cloths neatly folded, glass bottles arranged in careful rows, basins polished and waiting. Cassian checked them all, though he did not know why. It was not as if he could improve upon them by sheer will.

It wasn't the room he feared. It was the world beyond its door.

His hand trailed over the cradle he had built with Gideon's help all those years ago. It was made of sturdy oak, smooth as river stone where his thumb passed the curved edge. The smallest creak in the hall pulled his breath short. But it was just a false alarm.

He exhaled, rubbing both hands over his face. Time lost its shape.

Cassian could not have said whether an hour passed or five, only that the walls themselves seemed to breathe with tension. Every whisper beyond the bedchamber door made him stiffen. Every silence made him fear the worst.

When Lydia finally stepped into the corridor, her presence was a balm he had not known he needed. Her calm expression slowed his racing thoughts. She touched his arm briefly.

"She is doing well, Cassian," Lydia assured him. "Charlotte is brave and strong. She needs you to be the same."

He nodded, unable to speak just yet. Fear had lodged somewhere deep in his chest, like a jagged edge of a broken looking glass. Moments later, Nicholas arrived, already informed by a breathless footman. He entered with a rush of energy and, despite the gravity of the hour, managed a crooked grin.

"Well," Nicholas said, clapping Cassian on the shoulder, "if my sister has anything in common with me, she'll be finished in record time. Montclairs are efficient, after all."

It was absurd. And wholly inappropriate. Cassian nearly smiled.

But then a cry sounded from inside. It was Charlotte's voice, strained and fierce. Every muscle in his body seized. Without waiting for an invitation, Cassian pushed open the door and stepped in.

The room was warm, flickering with lamplight. The midwife stood at Charlotte's bedside, issuing gentle but firm instructions. Charlotte lay against the pillows. Her brow was damp with perspiration, and her breath was coming in determined bursts.

When she saw Cassian, her eyelashes fluttered. He was at her side in an instant. Charlotte reached for him with trembling fingers. He could see the exhaustion in her eyes. Cassian took her hand in both of his, grounding himself in the feel of her.

"I am here," he whispered, trying to keep control of himself and of the whole situation. "I'm not going anywhere."

Her eyes shone not with tears, but with courage. She nodded once, but her jaw set as another wave of pain overtook her. She bore it in silence at first, then with a low, breathy cry that tore at him far more than any wound he had ever taken.

"Breathe, my lady," the midwife instructed. "Slow and steady, good. Again, just so."

Cassian bent close, his forehead nearly touching Charlotte's.

"You're doing beautifully," he murmured. "I am so proud of you, so unbelievably proud."

She managed a weak laugh between breaths. "You... say that now..."

The next contraction ripped through her. Charlotte closed her eyes, fingers tightening around his so fiercely he felt it to his bones. Cassian braced her hand to his chest, as though he could siphon off her pain and bear it himself.

He watched her face pinched with strain, flushed with effort, and everything in him threatened to break. She was fighting for their child with a strength he had never fully understood until this moment. She was formidable, radiant, and all-powerful. And he, Cassian Oberon, a man feared in Parliament and respected by lords twice his age, had never felt so small, so humbled and so *utterly human.*

"I love you," he said, voice cracking as she pushed through another wave of agony. "I love you, Charlotte. You are the bravest soul I have ever known."

Her fingers turned in his grip, clasping his hand even tighter.

"Don't leave," she whispered through clenched teeth.

"Never," he breathed. "Never."

He stayed holding her hand, whispering praise, bowing his head against hers each time pain crested and receded. His heart ached with helpless awe as she fought, as she laboured, as she endured what he could not shield her from.

He had never admired anyone more. He had never loved anyone more. In that moment, Cassian understood that strength was not in battlefields or duels or titles. It was *here*, in this woman, in this bed, fighting through pain to bring hope into the world.

He kissed her knuckles. "You are my everything, Charlotte..."

Then, the world stopped. For one breathless instant, there was nothing: no sound, no motion, no air in his lungs. And then it came.

A thin, piercing cry filled the chamber, and Cassian's knees nearly gave way beneath him. His vision blurred as relief crashed over him so forcefully it stole his breath. He had not realized until that moment how tightly fear had strangled him from the inside.

"It's a girl," the midwife announced gently. "A strong one."

Charlotte collapsed back against the pillows, tears streaking her cheeks. She was pale, utterly spent, yet in Cassian's eyes she had never been more radiant.

A daughter. Their daughter.

Cassian pressed a trembling kiss to Charlotte's forehead, unable to speak. She reached weakly for his sleeve and smiled in a soft, exhausted curve of the lips that undid him completely.

"Go," she whispered. "Meet her."

He almost protested. He didn't want to leave Charlotte's side even for a moment, but she nodded again, encouraging him. Slowly, he turned toward the midwife, who approached with a swaddled bundle nestled in her arms.

Cassian reached out, and the moment the child was placed against his chest, something in him shattered. She was impossibly tiny, and warm, and real. Her cries softened as he held her close, with one broad palm cradling her small back, and the other supporting her head. He stared, awestruck, at the delicate features scrunching her face: the smallest mouth, the faintest lashes, skin flushed and new as dawn.

Cassian swallowed hard. His voice, when it came, was only a whisper.

"My daughter."

The words trembled in the air. He looked at Charlotte, and his heart nearly broke with gratitude so fierce it hurt. She watched him through half-lidded eyes, tears still glistening. Pride and love were shining through her exhaustion.

"She is perfect," Charlotte whispered.

Cassian nodded, unable to answer past the tightness in his throat. He stepped back to Charlotte's side and carefully lowered onto the edge of the bed so she could see the child more closely. Charlotte reached out, brushing one fingertip against the baby's cheek, gently and reverently.

Cassian bowed his head, pressing his lips to their daughter's brow. A tear escaped despite his effort to contain it, falling onto the blanket. He did not wipe it away.

Too many emotions collided within him: relief so profound it felt like collapse; gratitude sharp enough to wound; awe that bordered on disbelief. And beneath all of it, fierce, unyielding protectiveness roared into life.

He had been afraid of everything, afraid to hope, afraid to love, afraid to lose. But now, holding his child and seeing Charlotte safe, Cassian understood the truth with clarity that left him trembling: love was a risk worth taking. He would protect them both with his name, his strength, his breath, and his very soul until his last heartbeat.

Gently, he lowered their daughter into Charlotte's arms. When the midwife stepped back and the room settled into a hush, Charlotte lifted her gaze to Cassian.

"I have chosen a name," she said softly.

Cassian leaned closer, his heart thudding, though he did not know why. "Tell me."

Charlotte looked down at the child, brushing a curl of impossibly fine hair from her forehead. "Clara Eleanor," she whispered. "Clara, for brightness and clarity. Eleanor... to *remember* the joy, not the sorrow."

He swallowed and nodded. "Clara Eleanor Oberon." He tasted the name, savouring every syllable. "It is perfect."

A knock sounded before the door opened, and Lydia slipped in, her eyes shining the instant she saw the swaddled bundle in Charlotte's arms.

"Oh, she is beautiful," Lydia breathed, hurrying to the bedside. "May I?"

"At a distance," Cassian said, still fiercely protective.

Lydia laughed outright. "You act as though I intend to steal her. I only wish to admire!"

Nicholas followed close behind, folding his arms with a grin. "Well. She takes after my side, obviously. Look at that expression, she already thinks herself superior to us all."

Charlotte let out a tired laugh. Lydia swatted Nicholas' arm lightly, and he feigned injury, muttering something about being unappreciated in his own family.

But Cassian barely heard them.

Their voices faded into the background. It was all pleasant noise and warm laughter, yet distant. His world had shrunk to a very small circle: Charlotte, resting against his shoulder; Clara, asleep in her mother's arms; the steady rhythm of two heartbeats that mattered more than his own.

He sat beside them, one arm around Charlotte, the other resting protectively on the blanket. His daughter's tiny features drew his eyes again and again in wonder: the delicate lashes, the small bow of her mouth, the rise and fall of her chest.

He felt... *complete.*

It was a word he had never trusted and a feeling he had never expected to claim. Grief had once carved a hollow in him so deep he thought it could never be filled. Yet here, life had quietly crept in and planted something new.

I will not fail them.

The vow formed without ceremony, without sound, but with iron resolve.

Charlotte shifted slightly, leaning into him, her head nestling against his shoulder. He kissed her temple, letting gratitude sweep through him.

"Cassian?" she murmured with her eyes half-closed.

"Yes, my love?"

"Thank you for staying and for being here."

He tightened his embrace. "There is nowhere else I will ever be."

Clara sighed in her sleep, a small, contented sound as if she, too, understood she was safe. The husband, the wife, and the daughter remained like that, wrapped in lamplight and new life.

The storm had passed. The ghosts were gone. Now, in their place rested something fragile, precious, and full of promise.

THE END

Also by Valentina Lovelace

Thank you so much for reading **"To Tame the Dark Duke"**!

I hope you savoured every moment! If you did, you're welcome to explore **my full Amazon Book Catalogue here:**

https://go.valentinalovelace.com/bc-authorpage

Thank you for helping me bring my dream to life! ♥

Printed in Dunstable, United Kingdom